Advance Praise For
A Cry From Egypt

"I seriously have no words that can properly explain everything awesome about this book. The author, Hope Auer, is a young Christian woman who has an overwhelmingly amazing writing talent! *A Cry From Egypt* is a story like no other I have read."

– Dawn Winters, "Guiding Light Homeschool"

"I have worked as a writing teacher and editor for my entire adult life. I have read more stories from young authors than I can count, but **Hope's work is the first to make me think of JRR Tolkien, CS Lewis, and Frank Peretti when I read it.**"

– Patsy Brekke, "Mrs. B's Bonnet" at WritingFoundations.com

"Hope Auer… achieved the seemingly impossible; in *A Cry From Egypt*, she's written historically (and Biblically) accurate Christian fiction that leaps off the page and captivates the imagination as well as any secular tale… **This is exactly the type of writing that the Christian fiction genre needs.** Not fiction that is preachy, not fiction that is blatant and obvious, not fiction that has a few token things thrown in to make it "seem" Christian – but **fiction that has a Christian heart and soul.**"

– Shawna Bradley, "Tenacity Divine"

"In addition to accurate historical content, I enjoyed knowing that Hope had begun this book when she was a child herself. Reading a book about what children would have experienced from a child's point of view is enlightening. I hope that even more than learning about history, that **it has made my children think about their own faith, about the identity of the God we worship, and about their place in His plan.**"

– Debra Haagen, "Note-able Scraps"

"*A Cry from Egypt* is **one of the best Christian historical fiction novels I have ever read.** I am not exaggerating one bit."

– Hope Jackson, "Homeschooling 3"

"**I highly recommend it for all families** — families that enjoy engaging read-alouds, students wanting to take a closer look at the story of the Israelites' redemption from Egyptian bondage, or homeschoolers looking to add a greater depth of understanding to their Biblical history studies."

– Cristi Schwamb, "Through the Calm and Through the Storm"

"My youngest and I read *A Cry From Egypt* and both enjoyed the story. It was **a book that neither of us could put down easily.** Not only does it follow the Biblical account accurately but it adds another dimension to the account making us think more about what happened during that time in history."

– Barbara Campbell, "Alive in Spirit"

"Throughout the story we experience what it was like to actually be there when the plagues were sent. Seeing Aaron and Moses, hearing them tell Pharaoh to "Let the people go". **I cannot describe the feeling that came over me while reading this book. You must get this book and read it with your children.** They will be talking about this for days to come."

– Jan Brandes, "Reflections in the Window"

"**The story really brings the events of Exodus alive!** Jarah's struggle with her faith in the midst of her people's captivity is realistic, and the relation of each plague to a particular Egyptian god is deftly woven into the story and dialogue."

– Kara Haschke, "Home With Purpose"

"*A Cry from Egypt* brought new perspective to my reading of the Exodus account in Scripture. **Good fiction is not just entertaining but enlightening, too. This book met that expectation.** It just seemed to add flesh to the bones of the story. Moses is seen from a distance, but the true focus is on Jarah's family and the struggles of slavery. You know, I've read the story from Exodus many times. I never stopped and imagined just what it was like for the Israelite families. Perspective is everything."

– Laura Lane, "Harvest Lane Cottage"

"I've said it before and I must say it again. This is my heart's desire to see my children draw near to our Heavenly Father. **I want them to knew the power of GOD and feel His love for them. A Cry From Egypt helps us do just that.**"

– Lynn McInnis, "This Day Has Great Potential"

A Cry From Egypt

A Cry From Egypt

Book One of The Promised Land

BY
HOPE AUER

ILLUSTRATED BY
MIKE SLATON

GREAT WATERS PRESS
MAKING BIBLICAL FAMILY LIFE PRACTICAL

A Cry From Egypt

This book is a work of fiction. References to historic events, real people, or real locales are used fictitiously. Other names, characters, places, or incidents are the products of the author's imagination, and any resemblance to actual events or locales or persons, living or dead, are purely coincidental.

Scripture quotations taken from the New American Standard Bible® Copyright © 1960, 1962, 1963, 1968, 1971, 1972, 1973, 1975, 1977, 1995 by The Lockman Foundation. Used by permission. (www.Lockman.org)

Text copyright © 2013 Hope Auer. Art, illustrations, and design copyright © 2013 Great Waters Press. All rights reserved.

Printed and bound in the United States of America. All rights reserved. No part of this publication may be reproduced or transmitted in any form or by any means, electronic or mechanical, including photocopying, recording, or by an information storage and retrieval system, with the exception of a reviewer who may quote brief passages in a review to be printed in a newspaper or magazine, without written permission from the publisher. For information, contact Great Waters Press at info@GreatWatersPress.com.

Publisher's Cataloging-in-Publication Data
Auer, Hope, 1992.
   A Cry From Egypt./ Hope Auer
   p. cm.
   ISBN-10: 1-938554-01-9 (trade paperback)
   ISBN-13: 978-1-938554-01-8 (trade paperback)
Egypt – History – To 332 B.C. – Fiction …. 2. Illustrated by Mike Slaton. II. Title.
PZ7. A94 AC 2013 [Fic]
Library of Congress Control Number: 2012954104

Dedicated to my father, Ken Auer, who instilled in me a love for writing, a love for history, and a love for my Lord and Savior, Jesus Christ, who has truly delivered me.

And to the rest of my family:
My mom, who reviewed my book and encouraged me through this long process;
And my brothers, Caleb and Joshua, who patiently listened to my crazy ideas, and helped me develop my characters.

Contents

Preface	v
Rameses	1
Jarah's Question	9
What Happened at the Nile River?	21
Triumphs and Trials	37
Frogs?	47
"Thank you."	65
Whose God is Real?	79
A Hardened Heart	89
Ada	109
"Will We Ever Be Free?"	121
Broken Hearts	127
Back in the Palace	135
Trapped in the Darkness	139
Before the Pharaoh	153
The Passover	157
The Promised Land	167
My Research	177
Acknowledgments	181
Pronunciation Guide	185

PREFACE

This book is Christian historical fiction. So while the plagues and other events are things that really happened, Jarah and her family and friends are completely fictional characters. The things that Jarah and her family went through could have happened but we can't go back in time and see how the Egyptians treated their slaves or how all of the Israelites reacted to the plagues. But we do know that what the Bible says is true.

My goal in writing this book was to give others a glimpse into the lives of people who were impacted by God's awesome power—for good or for bad—and to encourage others in their faith. When I was a twelve-year-old girl I struggled with knowing who I believed in and why. As my faith grew and I became solid in my love and devotion for God, I knew that many other boys and girls still struggle with the same things that I went through. And unfortunately, there aren't many books out there that really encourage young adults and point them towards Christ. I am constantly appalled by so-called Christian fiction. I picked up a Christian historical fiction book in the bookstore about a year ago and started to skim through it. I was shocked. The content of the book was anything *but* Christian. The only Christian thing about it was that the word "God" was mentioned a couple of times. God doesn't just want your respect. He wants your heart. He desires that all should come to be saved. And I wanted children, young adults, and adults to be able to read something that would encourage them and inspire them to spend more time in the Word studying God's plan for the world and His plan for His Chosen People.

I pray that as you read this book you will see this Bible story in ways that you've never seen it before. I have stayed as true to the Biblical account and historical account as I could. I also tried to show the heart of God and the nature of man: how God sees things that we don't see, and how God is constantly asking us to draw near to Him. I used verses from the Bible as Moses speaks to the pharaoh, described the plagues as best as I could from the Biblical account, and used the Biblical names for the capital city of Egypt and land surrounding it. I did extensive research on other parts of the book where the Bible was lacking in detail. For example, we know that the Israelites were slaves. We know generally what kind of work they did. We don't know exactly how well they were treated but we do know that they had foremen and overseers. It's a strong possibility that some of the Israelites did indeed adopt the beliefs of the Egyptians, as shown by their worship of the Golden Calf later on in Exodus (Egyptians thought that cattle were sacred). So I've tried my best to not only stay true to the Bible, but true to history.

In the back of this book is a section with more of my research on the land, Pharaohs, clothing, architecture, and so on. I hope that it will answer any questions you have as your read further into the pages. And I pray that this book will instill a desire in you to delve deeper into your study of the scriptures and help you develop a love for His story. Thank you for reading! May you be blessed and inspired by Jarah's story.

RAMESES

Jarah ran down the dark, narrow street. Her breath was coming in short, painful gasps and her legs felt like they were made of putty. Tired as she was, she could not let the Egyptians soldiers get her. The fear of being beaten—or worse—pushed her onwards. Staggering into an alleyway surrounded by stone houses, Jarah tried to quiet her breathing. She easily slid into a tiny hiding place behind a barrel. Jarah drew in a sharp breath as she heard the pounding of soldiers' feet and their angry voices.

"Where is she?"

"She couldn't have gotten away."

"The little tramp!"

A guard was barking orders. "You three head down the street. The rest of you, spread out and search the side roads. We'll catch that little thief."

A shadow darkened the entrance to the side-street in which Jarah was hiding. She bit her lip. Her whole body was trembling. Walking through the alley, the Egyptian guard peered about sharply. Jarah pulled her legs up to her chest and tried to shield herself with her basket. She held her breath until her lungs ached, praying that the soldier wouldn't find her.

After looking around, the man shrugged and began to walk away. Relief swept over Jarah, but it came too soon. As the guard walked past her, the sword which hung by his side struck the barrel. The barrel was empty and toppled over. Impulsively, Jarah reached out to grab it. The soldier saw her. An exclamation of surprise came from his lips. He jerked the barrel away.

"I've found her," the soldier bellowed.

"Please sir—" Jarah began, but was interrupted when the soldier caught a handful of her hair. He yanked Jarah to her feet. Jarah screamed and struggled but was dragged out to the main street. She was thrown down before a broad, sneering Egyptian who held a long whip. More soldiers seemed to pour out of the shadows and surround her.

"What are you doing here after curfew, girl?" the man with the whip demanded.

"Please, please sir—" Jarah pleaded as tears of pain gathered in her eyes and obscured her vision. Before she could say more she felt the whip hit her back with tremendous force. Jarah barely kept herself from falling on her face.

"What were you doing here?" the man shouted.

"I was bringing linen to the queen!" Jarah exclaimed. "My mother, Mariel, is in charge of making linen for the queen."

"A likely story," the Egyptian snorted.

"No! I'm telling the truth. Ask the queen!" Jarah practically screamed.

No one listened to her plea. The whip struck her back again and again. The soldiers around Jarah laughed and mocked her pain. Jarah bit her lip so hard that she tasted blood. Soon she could hold back the screams no longer. Her shrill cry pierced the still air. She began to feel light-headed, and then the blows stopped. Someone was shaking her.

"No, please. Leave me alone," Jarah begged, weakly.

"Jarah. Jarah."

"Huh? What?" Jarah sat up, panting and wet with sweat. Her mother's eyes were staring into hers.

"It's morning. The foreman will be here any minute. You've overslept. Get some breakfast," Mother ordered angrily.

"Yes, Mother," Jarah replied. Her heart was racing, but relief washed over her like a wave.

It was only a nightmare, she told herself, releasing a shaky breath. *Only a nightmare...*

א

Jarah dashed down the street, clutching a basket filled with linen. Turning a corner in the dusty road, she saw a group of Israelite men pulling a wagon full of bricks. They were straining hard at the ropes, their muscles tight and flexing. An older man's legs suddenly gave out and he collapsed.

"Up! Up, you fool!" the overseer commanded. But the man couldn't rise.

"Up I said!" the overseer yelled. He pulled a whip from his belt and began to beat the man. Jarah gasped. The man cried out, begging for mercy. But the fierce whine of the whip and the terrified screams didn't stop. Jarah wanted to cover her ears. She pressed herself up against a stone building, trying to edge around the overseer and avoid his whip. Finally she passed the horrible scene and ran into the city of Rameses. The streets were growing dark.

Oh no, Jarah panicked. *It's getting late. I'm late in delivering the cloth again. What'll they do to Mother?* Jarah forced herself to run as fast as her sore legs would carry her. She had to get to the palace fast before their family was punished. Tears of worry and weariness threatened to spill out of Jarah's eyes. She blinked them back.

I hate being a slave. I've been a slave for twelve years. I want to be free. I want my family to be free without any Egyptians around threatening to beat us or punish us. It just isn't fair! she thought angrily. Her father said that the Israelites had been slaves to the Egyptians for over four hundred years and the Egyptians just kept getting crueler.

Why can't they treat us like normal people? Jarah struggled up one of the steeply sloped streets.

She looked up briefly to gauge where the sun was in the sky. The sun was just beginning to sink behind the capital city. Turning around, Jarah saw the land of Goshen behind her falling into shadow.

If I hurry, maybe everything will be fine. Maybe Ada will be waiting for me and can smooth things over, Jarah thought as she started to run again.

Jarah kept in the shadows of the tall buildings, eyes always alert. She didn't want to be caught by any Egyptian guards. Usually her brothers came with her and there was nothing to worry about. But tonight Eitan and Lemuel had been kept late at work and Jarah had been made to go to the city alone.

Suddenly around a bend in the road, some Egyptian soldiers appeared, well-armed and coming towards her. Jarah looked frantically for a place to hide. There was a side-street and she dashed into it, panting and wheezing. She saw a wooden barrel and slumped down behind it. A sudden thought struck Jarah. She gulped hard.

This is exactly what happened in my nightmare. Please oh please don't let it come true. Jarah curled her feet and legs underneath her. *I hope they didn't see me.* The frayed edge of her dress brushed the dirty road as she pulled the basket closer to her, trying to make herself as small as possible.

The men's voices came closer. Jarah's heart was thumping in her ears so loudly that Jarah thought the soldiers would hear it and find her. Briefly their figures appeared, shooting ominous silhouettes down the alleyway. Jarah held her breath to keep from screaming. To her utter astonishment the soldiers continued on their way, not even looking in her direction. Slowly Jarah exhaled in great relief, stood up, and then crept out of hiding and continued down the main street.

Dusk was quickly approaching and the sunset painted the sand dunes on the distant horizon in a rainbow of colors while Jarah struggled up the slight hill on which the palace rested. She hurried around a corner of the outer wall and came to the servants' entrance. Two guards stood outside of it. Nausea welled up in Jarah's stomach as she approached the guards. But the guards barely noticed her and let her enter with a grunt of welcome. They knew what errand she was on. Jarah tried to still her heavy breathing and pushed the heavy door open. She slipped in and the gate closed behind her with a resounding *bang*.

Inside the protective palace walls Jarah jogged through a small but lavish courtyard. Water trickled from numerous fountains; flowers perfumed the air. Rich and colorful couches and cushions littered the ground. Jarah ran through the garden and came to the wooden door which led into the kitchen. But then she stopped in her tracks. Ada wasn't there.

Where is she? Did she forget to come get the linen? She doesn't usually forget. Jarah was left with no other choice but to knock on the door. She timidly lifted her hand and knocked. For several sickening minutes nothing happened. Abruptly, the door was pulled open and Jarah was thrilled to see Ada step out into the pale, evening light.

"Jarah? What are you doing here alone?" Ada asked in surprise. Her friend's slim, graceful figure was covered in a white linen dress which glowed in the fading sunlight. Her rich brown curls framed her beautiful, loving face. But though Ada had a smile on her lips, her dark eyes seemed fearful and uneasy.

"I had to come alone. Everyone else was working," Jarah replied. "But here's the cloth. I'm sorry I'm late."

Ada took the cloth from the basket, her gold bracelets tinkling as she said, "It's quite all right. I'll keep your family from trouble. I wish I could have someone escort you back to your house since it's getting dark, but there's trouble in the court. We have some visitors here to see the pharaoh, and though I would love to stay and talk I'm afraid I must get back to the queen. She's been fretting all day and I'm the only maid she will turn to for comfort."

"Do you have a message for your family that you want me to bring back?" Jarah asked.

Ada nodded, making her ringlets bounce as a slight smile spread across her lips. "Tell them I'm fine and that I'm seeing Yahweh at work in Egypt at last. They—and you—will see what I mean soon enough. Good-night." And with a quick parting smile, Ada reentered the palace and closed the door.

"I wonder what Ada meant by that," Jarah pondered aloud as she made her way back out to the street. She repeated Ada's message over and over to herself, trying to remember every word to pass on to Ada's family and her own. Ada hardly ever got to go home and she relied on Jarah and her brothers to tell her own family what was going on in the palace.

As Jarah ran past a row of rich houses she heard a lovely voice singing a song. Slowing, she saw a small girl her own age sitting in a tiny, but exquisite courtyard. Vines grew over the small fence and the girl sat very daintily on a wooden stool, her hands folded and resting in her lap. Tiny reed sandals peeped out from beneath the hem of her white linen dress and she wore one golden bracelet on her thin wrist. She looked kindly into the face of a young boy about five years of age. The boy's head was shaved like every other Egyptian boy, except for a small patch of long black hair, and he wore a white skirt tied with a red cord. The boy was enraptured in his sister's song. Jarah smiled. They looked so happy and peaceful. That was what she wanted. Peace, and freedom.

Abruptly, Jarah's foot hit a stone and she tumbled forwards, very awkwardly, and landed hard on her hands and knees. She heard a voice call out, "Are you all right?"

Jarah looked up. The girl who had been singing was just reaching the gate. She looked concerned until she saw who Jarah was. Her piercing black eyes instantly hardened and she said, "Oh. You're a *Hebrew.*" She almost spat the word. "I thought you were someone else." The girl turned up her nose with an air of authority and disdain which made Jarah feel very uncomfortable.

Blinking back tears of embarrassment, Jarah slowly rose to her feet. Her right knee was stinging, but Jarah masked the pain and said, rather clumsily, "I... I'm sorry, young lady." She bowed her head in reverence.

The girl waved her hand dismissively. "You'd better go. It's almost curfew time. You could get turned in." The way the girl said "turned in" sent shivers up and down Jarah's spine.

"Yes, young lady," Jarah said, trying to be polite. She bowed her head again, snatched her basket, and took off down the street into the darkness. But she heard a little voice with a lisp behind her.

"Who was *that*, Acenith?"

"A slave girl, Bes. A Hebrew. You don't need to concern yourself with her," she said, in absolute disgust.

Tears flowed freely from Jarah's eyes now. She couldn't help but feel hurt.

She treated me like I didn't matter, like I was an—an animal. Jarah brushed tears from her eyes and glanced down at her throbbing knee. She saw a trickle of blood spill down her calf.

You're so dumb and clumsy! You'll never amount to anything! You'll never be pretty and wealthy like her! Jarah yelled inwardly. Her throat constricted as she tried to stop her bitter sobs. She couldn't think about it anymore. She just had to get home.

Jarah ran, barely seeing anything through the blur of tears. Her chest was heaving, but Jarah didn't want to stop. She couldn't stop. She needed to get home. But just then, an arm shot out of the darkness and clutched her shoulder. Gasping in horror, Jarah felt panic rush into her heart like a flood. She tried to pull away but the hand tightened its grip on her arm.

Come on, Jarah. You can get out of this, she told herself, struggling and kicking. But the vice-like grip tightened and Jarah knew there was no escape. She spun around to face her opponent, terror written all over her face as she stared up into angry black eyes.

A CRY FROM EGYPT

JARAH'S QUESTION

"What are you doing here, slave? Snooping about, are you?" an Egyptian soldier barked. "No Hebrews are allowed in the city at this time of day."

"No, sir. Honestly, I haven't done anything wrong. Please let me go." Jarah squirmed and tried to pull away.

The soldier laughed raucously at her struggles and then commanded her, "Hold still. What do you have in that basket?"

"Nothing. I just had to bring some fabric to the palace. Please let me go!" Jarah repeated, getting frantic now. There was no one to help her. Her mind spun as she remembered scenes from her dream the night before.

"Give me that basket."

Jarah shoved the basket towards him and though the soldier found nothing in it, he still did not appear pleased. He looked into her face searchingly as he said, "It's quite suspicious that you should be running around the streets alone at night." The Egyptian no longer seemed fierce but quizzical, as if he was trying to determine whether or not

Jarah was telling the truth. "You'll have to be questioned further," he finally stated. And with that the soldier dragged her out of the alley and into the street, back towards the palace.

No! What if I get beaten? I'll never be able to get back home. And how will my family find me? What did I do wrong? Why won't he listen to me? Jarah thought, panicking.

Just then a voice called out, "Sir? Where are you taking my sister?"

Jarah's head spun around and the Egyptian stopped in his tracks. Jarah saw with relief the strong, slender figure of her fourteen-year-old brother, Lemuel. He was coming to her rescue.

"Lemuel, help!" Jarah yelled. Lemuel's eyes quickly shot her a glance that told her to remain calm.

"So this is your sister?" the Egyptian asked with a smirk. "I'm taking her to be questioned by the authorities."

"Did she do something wrong?" Lemuel asked, politely.

"I'm just taking her to be questioned," the Egyptian replied with some annoyance, starting to move on again.

Lemuel took a step forward. "Sir, my sister came here to deliver some cloth to the Queen. It's our family's duty to bring this cloth to her regularly. My mother's name is Mariel, wife of Asher of the tribe of Asher." The Egyptian stopped and his eyes stared penetratingly into Lemuel's, trying to determine the truth. Jarah heard footsteps behind her.

"Mubariz, leave these children alone." A young Egyptian man approached them.

"And why should I, Paki?" Mubariz asked.

"What the boy says is true," Paki asserted. "I've seen members of their family come to the palace regularly with cloth for the queen."

"Very well." Mubariz shrugged a little reluctantly and released his strong grip on Jarah's arm. She bounded over to Lemuel and he moved his arm in front of her protectively as the soldier moved back to his post and out of sight. Paki approached them.

"Thank you, sir," Lemuel said respectfully. Jarah nodded to him in reverence. She could see from the clothes Paki wore, the way he carried himself, and the golden band around his wrist that this Egyptian was a very wealthy servant.

"It was nothing," Paki replied with a slight smile. "Now you'd better go home. It's getting late."

"Yes sir." Lemuel nodded and Paki headed off towards a row of rich houses.

"Jarah, are you all right?" Lemuel's face showed great concern as he faced his younger sister.

"I'm fine, Lemuel," Jarah answered.

"Are you sure? Your leg's bleeding."

"Yes. Really, I'm fine. I just tripped and fell." Before Lemuel could ask anything else she hastened to say, "Where's Father and Eitan?"

"They're still at work. Father's back has been bothering him all day so he's moving a little slower, and Eitan's helping him finish up. But Father sent me to bring you home since I'm done and it's getting dark," Lemuel replied, the look of concern and worry now dissolving from his brow.

"Well I'm glad you're here," Jarah said, shifting the woven basket under her arm.

"Here, let me take that," Lemuel said with a kind smile.

Jarah handed the basket over to him with a murmured "Thank you," and an affectionate smile up into her brother's face.

"How was work?" Lemuel queried.

"Good. I was cleaning out the temple of Ra today. It wasn't so bad because we were wet and working in the shade. But the overseer was really particular."

Lemuel laughed at the irritated expression on Jarah's face. "I'm sure you did a great job, as usual," Lemuel assured her, graciously.

They walked on for a little while in silence. Both were very tired from their long day of work. Jarah's arm was sore from where the Egyptian had grabbed her. She rubbed it gently with her other hand and sighed deeply.

"Lemuel, why are all the Egyptians so mean?" Jarah asked.

Lemuel laughed. "Not all Egyptians are mean, Jarah."

"What?" Jarah's jaw dropped open in surprise at Lemuel's answer.

"That one who stopped you tonight wasn't."

"What?" Jarah was shocked. "You don't think he was mean?"

"No. He wasn't. He was just doing his job. He didn't beat you or hurt you did he?" Lemuel prodded.

"No... At least, not much," Jarah answered, hesitantly and quietly.

"He was just taking you away because he thought you might be lying. But then he found out that you were telling the truth and he left you alone instead of beating you for no reason. Not all Egyptians are cruel and bitter, Jarah. Some are actually very kind. Remember, several families offer to give us food and other things when we need them. Just because a few Egyptians are mean doesn't mean that every Egyptian is. And you know the Egyptians' so-called 'gods' are very cruel. So they've basically been taught to be mean. They don't know the truth. They don't know about Yahweh's mercy and love. Truth can make all the difference in a person's life, Jarah. Remember that."

"How do you know all that, Lemuel?" Jarah questioned in awe.

Lemuel smiled and his deep brown eyes twinkled. "I asked Father a very similar question not too long ago. Father has taught me a lot about Yahweh and about the world around us. You should talk to Father whenever you have questions, Jarah. I'm sure with Yahweh's help he'll be able to answer them," Lemuel replied, wisely.

"But I don't know. Father's always so tired, and—"

"Jarah, he's never too tired to talk to us." Lemuel's voice was very soft and gentle. He looked down at his little sister and suddenly stated, "You're scared of him, aren't you?"

"Well, maybe a little," Jarah admitted in a low voice. "He's just so wise. And, I mean, I don't want him to think I'm a silly girl who can't figure anything out by myself."

"But that's what fathers are there for, Jarah, to help us figure things out and to guide us and answer our questions." The siblings walked quietly for a few more moments before Lemuel finished, "You should talk to him, Jarah."

Jarah just nodded. She wanted to, very badly. She could just hope she had enough courage to reveal her heart to her father, just as she had done to Lemuel.

I guess the reason why I'm so uncomfortable around Father is because he believes in Yahweh. I'm not sure if I do. I mean, in some things Yahweh seems to be there. But other times, He's not. And if He was really there, why are we in slavery? Maybe Yahweh does really hear my prayers and just doesn't answer them right away. Or… maybe it's just coincidence and there's no God at all?

They were now entering Goshen. The last rays of the setting sun still lit up the poor, dirty town. They turned a corner in the road and saw their small mud hut in the midst of many others. In front of it was Jarah's beautiful older sister, Shayna. She was watching their younger brothers, Raphael and Yanni, who were five and two. But something didn't seem right. Raphael and Yanni weren't laughing and running. They were sitting close to Shayna on a small bench, looking pale and nervous. Shayna looked up and saw them, and a look of relief spread across her formerly tight face.

"Oh no," Lemuel breathed.

"What? What's wrong?" Jarah demanded.

Then she heard it. A shrill, angry voice from inside the hut. Jarah immediately felt her body tense up. "Oh no," she muttered under her breath. "Mother's at Father, again."

"There you two are," Shayna hissed. "What took you so long?"

"We got stopped by a soldier, but we're all right," Lemuel assured her, softly. "What's going on inside?"

Before Shayna could answer Tirzah, Jarah's eight-year-old sister, poked her head out of the door. Her face was almost white and tears brimmed in her amber eyes.

"Lemuel. Jarah," she squealed in delight. She ran towards them and threw her arms around Lemuel, burying her curly head in his chest. Her body trembled with sobs.

"Shh. It's all right. Everything will be fine," Lemuel whispered, holding his little sister close.

It must be a pretty bad argument if Tirzah's this upset, Jarah thought with a shudder.

Shayna came closer and lowering her voice she said, "It started when Father came back late again. Mother's been frustrated by how Father hasn't been home much. You know she gets tired really easily and Jarah and I have been working even more than usual. But, I think she's really mad because he's been spending so much time with Eitan talking to him about Yahweh. She thinks Father's indoctrinating him and not letting him make his own decisions about who he believes in. And to be perfectly honest, I think she's right."

"Shayna," Lemuel said, a little defensively, "it's not all Father's fault. Work's been hard. And Eitan's trying to make some very important decisions about his future. And if Mother's mad at Father for trying to 'indoctrinate' Eitan, I think she does the same thing to everyone else, talking about how the only gods are the Egyptian gods. But so far, I haven't seen any Egyptian gods show any power at all."

Shayna shifted her weight uncomfortably and rolled her eyes. But she managed to retort, "Well, I haven't seen Yahweh show any power, either."

Lemuel looked penetratingly at Shayna. Jarah could feel the tension between them.

"Shayna," Lemuel began slowly, "don't you remember? Four years ago, when you were eleven, Mother didn't make enough linen for our weekly quota. The overseer was furious and beat Mother. We thought she was going to die. Don't you remember?"

Shayna's face was pale and her eyes were fixed on the ground as she murmured, "Yes. Of course I do."

Jarah squinted her eyes shut. Why did Lemuel have to bring that up? It was a memory she had tried so hard to erase from her mind…

א

Jarah stood next to Lemuel, pressed against the wall. The big man was hitting her mother. He was hitting her over and over again. He was hitting her with his whip and with his fists. Why didn't he stop? Why was he hitting her? Mother was on the ground now, but she didn't cry out. The man hit her again, and this time she turned away from the blow. Her mother's back was covered in blood. Jarah gasped. She was shaking like a leaf. Shayna was in the corner, huddled over little Tirzah and Raphael, screaming and crying and begging for mercy. Then Jarah heard her mother cry out. A wild, inhuman scream of terror and pain. Jarah's heart stopped beating. She froze, too shocked even to scream. The man was on the ground, pounding her with his fists, shouting, "You've been late one time too many! Now you're getting what you deserve, filthy Hebrew!"

"Stop! Stop! Please!" Shayna was shrieking.

Mother screamed again. The man continued to hit her. Jarah suddenly realized he was trying to kill her. Then Mother's screams grew softer and softer. Jarah saw her face turn gray.

"NO! STOP!" She heard the blood-curtailing yell, barely recognizing it as her own.

"Stop it! You're going to kill her!" Lemuel cried out.

Jarah was too numb to think, see, or move. Through tear-filled eyes she saw Lemuel charge the evil man who was three times his size. He tackled the man, but the man simply slung him into the wall, effortlessly. Jarah heard someone scream her name.

"Jarah! Go find Father! GO!"

Shayna's command jerked Jarah out of her shock. Everything was blurry, but she ran. She ran as fast as she could out the door. She ran, looking for her father. She didn't stop. She couldn't stop. She had to find Father. She ran, for how long she didn't know. She ran to the river, to the temple, to the mud pits, in and out of groups of working Hebrews. She barely noticed her own fatigue until she was back at the house. But she hadn't found Father. Where was he? What could she do? She hadn't found him. In panic she dashed into the house. And then she instantly froze in mid-step. Her mother lay there on the floor, barely recognizable. She was covered in blood and bruises and her leg was twisted at a weird angle. And she wasn't moving.

Shayna was shrieking and wailing, but Jarah didn't hear what she was saying. She was absolutely stunned. She felt Lemuel's arms around her. He was shaking. She felt so dizzy, so shocked. Everything looked misty and dim and slowly faded into darkness…

ב

"Do you remember what you said, after the man left and you were trying to take care of Mother?" Lemuel pressed. Jarah opened her eyes and stared into Shayna's face.

"Not really." Shayna shrugged.

"You said, 'Yahweh, please, heal my Mother. Please, I beg you, heal her. Help me heal her. I don't want her to die.' And Yahweh gave you the wisdom. He told you what to do to bandage and take care of Mother. You saved her life. How can you say that Yahweh doesn't exist?"

Shayna's head was bowed in shame. But before she could say anything, Mother stuck her head out of the door. Her face was aflame with passion and her hazel eyes were snapping fire.

"There you two are! Jarah, get in here right now! I need help with dinner!" Mother barked. Then she was gone and Jarah heard her angry, shrill voice inside. She shrank back towards Lemuel.

"Do I have to go in there?" she whispered, pleadingly.

Lemuel gave her a half-smile. "Yes. You can do it. Just don't say anything and be helpful. Mother won't hurt you, you know that."

Jarah gathered up all of her courage and walked towards the door. *No*, she thought. *Mother's never hurt my body. But… she's hurt my heart.* She steeled herself for whatever she would find inside and pushed the door open.

In the dim hut, she saw her father sitting silently on a stool in the middle of the room. In the back of the hut, her eighteen-year-old brother Eitan sat in a dark corner, barely visible. Her mother was pacing the dirt floor, limping because of her deformed leg. And she was still yelling at Father.

"Asher, after all I've done for you and these children, all the hard work I do every day, I deserve to have a say in their religion. I slave here all day long, watching Yanni and Raphael, teaching them the ways of Ra, and you're out with Eitan somewhere indoctrinating him. You haven't even given him a chance to learn about the Egyptian gods. For the past ten years I've barely been able to see him. And now at this critical time in his life, I have no say in the matter!"

"Now Mariel—" Father began, but Mother interrupted him.

"No. You don't understand. You knew when we married that I had different views than you. You said that the arranged marriage would still work and that you'd let me have my say. Well, whenever I teach the children anything you go behind my back and teach them about your pathetic Yahweh. It's mean and weak of you to act that way!"

"Mariel, I'm sorry. I didn't know you felt that way. Let's just try to calm down and discuss this," Father said, making an effort to stay peaceful.

Jarah's Question

Jarah silently moved around the table putting out clay bowls while her Mother exploded, "Calm down? You want me to calm down? Asher, this is a matter of life and death! If Eitan doesn't accept the Egyptian gods there will be no after-life for him. You've made him believe in Yahweh and given him no choice in the matter. He's going to grow up embittered and weak. He's not going to make it into eternity. You need to let him be."

"Now Mariel, I—"

"Wait, Father." Eitan suddenly stood up and moved into the dim candlelight. Jarah thought that her brother looked very determined and strong. A gentle light filled his eyes. How could her mother think he would become a weak man?

"Mother, you say that Father is indoctrinating me. But what you haven't thought of is this: I want Father to tell me about Yahweh. I've done a lot of observing in the past eighteen years and I've come to the conclusion that Yahweh is the true God and that He gives a strength and peace that I've always longed for. He gives you the ultimate after-life. The Egyptian gods fill everyone with hatred and fear. I can't live that way. Yahweh has fulfilled my desires like no other god can. In fact, I believe there are no other gods. Father's giving me advice about moving forward in my decisions about marriage and life. I need his advice. If you have to blame anyone for this so called 'indoctrination,' blame me."

Eitan said all of this so quietly, but with such strength, that he had held everyone in the family spellbound. Eitan so rarely spoke that this strong argument was a shock to them all. Jarah suddenly realized that Mother had stopped pacing. Her father was sitting absolutely still, a pleased and surprised expression on his face. Jarah noticed that she was standing next to the table, holding a plate in her outstretched hand.

"Jarah, hurry up with it!" Mother shouted abruptly. Jarah jumped a little and rushed to finish the task of preparing for dinner. Mother cleared her throat and muttered, "Very well, Eitan. That excuses your father somewhat. Just see that you're teaching the children both sides, Asher. And stop going behind my back." She turned a dark look to Father.

"I will try to do better, Mariel," Father promised.

Mother stuck her nose up in the air in a superior way as if to say, "I've won this one," and went outside to bring everyone else in for dinner.

Even though the argument was over, dinner was eaten in almost complete silence. An angry, oppressive air could be felt in the house. Mother looked proud and confident. Father, though he still seemed determined and loving, did seem a little shaken. Eitan was, as usual, silent, though he and Shayna exchanged many uneasy glances. And everyone else didn't want to do anything or say anything that would bring up another disagreement.

Chores were finished quickly. Everyone was very helpful that night, even little Raphael and Yanni. Soon they all collapsed into bed, exhausted. Everyone, that is, except Father and Eitan, who still sat outside. Jarah could hear their voices borne into the house by the soft breeze. And though she couldn't make out what they were saying, their voices seemed to be calling to her. And instead of feeling more tired, she felt more and more awake. Lemuel's words kept coming back to her.

"You should talk to him, Jarah."

I know I should, but he's talking to Eitan now.

Jarah sighed and rolled over. Her eyes met Lemuel's. He was curled up with Raphael on their small cot. His eyes penetrated into hers and seemed to encourage her in her desire. Very quietly and gently, so as not to wake her bed-mate Tirzah, she got up and crept outside.

"Father?" Jarah asked, approaching him where he sat on a wooden bench next to Eitan.

"Yes, Jarah?" Father replied, caringly.

"Can I ask you something?" she shyly inquired. She rebuked herself for being so timid.

"Certainly," her father answered.

"Well, is… I mean, how do you know that Yahweh's really there? I mean, Lemuel was talking to me, and I just don't see why Yahweh would let us be in slavery like this. It just doesn't seem like He's around much at all, and that if He is, whatever He does could also be coincidence—couldn't it? And then… Oh! I don't know." Tears filled Jarah's eyes as she swallowed a sob.

Jarah's Question

"Jarah," her father began tenderly, "you're just at a time of questioning in your life." He smiled at Jarah and the smile dissolved some of her doubts and fears. Father continued, "I know that you are trying to sort things out and find out what is really right and true. I know that you listen to what I say about Yahweh and want to serve Him. But it is difficult. I know it is. Since you can't see Him, you can't always feel that Yahweh is there to help you. But He is, Jarah. You can see Him in all creation. Do you think those gods of stone the Egyptians serve could have created this world and all of these animals and people?"

"No," Jarah replied, giggling at the idea.

"No. Of course not. They have no power or wisdom. They're just blocks of wood and stone. But our God is above everything, Jarah. He is Lord of all. When I look carefully, I see Yahweh's many signs and wonders. Just look for Him more throughout your day and I know you'll find Him."

Jarah grinned at her Father as Eitan turned towards her and said quietly, "It's good you're asking questions, Jarah. It's right to know why you believe what you have been told to believe."

"Yes, you're doing the right thing," Father added. "Just keep trusting in Yahweh and praying to Him. And Jarah, I know that Yahweh will work all things out for good."

Then Jarah remembered Ada's message. *"They—and you—will see what I mean soon enough."* Jarah wondered… did Ada mean that she would see Yahweh at work? And soon? She wished she hadn't come back home so late so that she could have delivered the message to Ada's family.

"What are you thinking about?" her father asked her.

"Oh, I was just thinking about what Ada told me today. She told me to tell her family that she was seeing Yahweh at work. I wonder if we'll see Him work soon, too."

"Maybe we will," Father said with a smile, exchanging an understanding look with Eitan. Turning back to Jarah he said, "You should go to bed now. It's getting late."

"Yes sir. Thank you," Jarah said, even though she still didn't feel sleepy. She felt like she was floating on air. Just that simple reassurance of Yahweh's existence gave Jarah hope and comfort. She would do what Father said and perhaps her faith would grow in ways she couldn't even imagine.

"Oh Jarah? Make sure you help your mother as much as you can. I think I have been helping her more than she thinks, but she's been very tired recently. We all need to help her, even if it's hard. Do you understand?"

"Yes Father, I will. Good-night."

"Good-night," Father and Eitan answered.

As Jarah slipped underneath her sheet next to Tirzah, she offered a small prayer to God.

Yahweh, thank you for answering my prayers today for safety. Please make me more encouraging towards everybody, like Father, Eitan, and Lemuel. I really want to be better than I am and find out more about You and trust You more. I know that I made the decision to worship You when I was a little girl. But sometimes You just seem so far away, and it's so hard. And Yahweh? Please deliver us from the Egyptians and their gods. I don't want to serve them or their gods for the rest of my life. Please help us. Amen.

And gradually Jarah drifted off to sleep.

WHAT HAPPENED AT THE NILE RIVER

A ray of early morning sunlight stole into the little hut and gently fell onto Jarah's face, slowly awakening her. Wearily, she opened her eyes and looked around the dim room. No one else was awake. She could feel Tirzah stirring beside her and heard her little sister moan in her sleep.

Oh what I wouldn't give for a day to just rest, she thought with a small groan. Her muscles ached from yesterday's work.

Outside the door, Jarah could see her mother cooking something in the fire pit. The smell made Jarah hungry. She knew that there was no use in trying to go back to sleep. Stretching and yawning, she rose from the bed and stepped outside. The harsh sun against the white sand dunes in the distance stung her eyes. In front of Jarah, the nearby marshlands and the distant desert stretched out in all directions. A twisted band of silver wound its way through the sand and grass and fields: the Nile River. To her left was the crowded Hebrew town, filled with similar mud and brick buildings. On Jarah's right was the tall, magnificent city of Rameses. Jarah shielded her face with her calloused hand and tried to focus on her mother who was kneading bread dough next to the fire.

"Do you need any help, Mother?" Jarah asked. Her mother's face looked pained.

"Oh, there you are," her mother said, straightening her back. "I thought you were going to sleep the whole morning. Go wake the others. We don't have much time until Amasai comes and we still need to get water from the creek and eat something."

"Yes, Mother," Jarah responded, trying not to imitate Mother's exasperated tone.

When Jarah stepped inside to wake the others, she realized that Eitan and Father were gone. *Must've gone to the Nile to pray,* she thought.

Once everyone was up, Jarah started to set out the clay bowls for their breakfast while Lemuel, Tirzah, and Raphael went to a fork of the Nile River. They brought clothes to wash and pitchers to carry back water for the day.

As they left, Shayna came in from taking Yanni on his morning walk. Shayna took Yanni for a walk every morning as an excuse to waste his energy, but Jarah knew that Shayna also went to see some of her own friends. Shayna spent any spare time she had with three boys named Mayer, Yaphet, and Zephon. Jarah was disgusted by those three boys. They were lazy good for nothings, always looking for trouble, and very flirtatious. Jarah couldn't stand flirtatious people. And she also couldn't stand doing Shayna's work for her while she was out having fun. Why couldn't Shayna pick one of the nice boys who spent time with the elders like Eitan did? If Shayna had to spend all of her time with boys, why not pick one that was actually ready to get married? Jarah wished Shayna was more like Ada.

"There you are," Shayna said to Jarah in an irate fashion. "I was afraid you were still going to be asleep. Did you ask Mother if she needed any help?"

"Yes I did. Why wouldn't I?" Jarah mumbled sarcastically. Why did her sister always have to boss her around? Suddenly, Jarah noticed the tone in her voice and whispered, "I'm sorry, Shayna. I shouldn't have responded like that."

"Well hurry up," Shayna ordered, obviously not even considering making an apology of her own. "Amasai will be here in just a few minutes and we'll have to get to work, with or without food." Her sister's tone hadn't changed but Jarah was able to suffocate the harsh feelings that were now rising in her chest as she turned back to finish putting out the wooden utensils.

In a few minutes, Lemuel, Tirzah, and Raphael came back to the hut with the wet clothes and drinking water. Tirzah was also helping Mother carry in a pot of porridge. Everyone took their places at the table as their mother looked outside worriedly.

"Everyone start eating. I don't know where your father and brother are, but we don't have time to waste. They'll just have to miss breakfast," Mother instructed. To herself she muttered resentfully, "And after everything I said to him last night, too."

Lemuel took the initiative to pray to Yahweh in very intimate tones and thanked Him for the food. They had just started eating when their father and Eitan returned hurriedly.

"At last," said mother in a scolding tone. "You're late again and Amasai will be here any minute to give us our tasks for the day."

"I'm sorry, Mariel. We were praying and the time passed so quickly." Father shared a knowing smile with Eitan and then greeted the rest of his children. Eitan also said "Good-morning" to his siblings and then sat down and devoured the hunk of bread and porridge set before him. In Eitan's eyes there shown that light of peace and love that always came from his talks with Father.

"After everything I said to you last night, encouraging you to be home more and let me have time with Eitan, you still persist in being late," Mother grumbled.

Father stopped eating long enough to reply with some annoyance, "We were also discussing what to do to help you around the house, Mariel."

"Oh." Mother seemed slightly taken aback. But she caught herself quickly and stated, "I'm glad you're actually thinking of me."

They had barely finished eating when Amasai, the Israelite foreman, strode into the house. He had a scowl on his tan face.

"I'm afraid you won't have time to clean up from breakfast," he began. "Our work load has been doubled. We need to get moving."

Everyone gasped.

"Doubled?!" Mother exploded. "Why? For what reason?"

Amasai sighed and shook his head. "Last night there was a huge uproar in the palace. I'm sure since you all are so involved with deliveries to the palace that you've heard rumors and stories about the lost prince?"

Jarah nodded. She had heard many people mention the lost prince named Moses. Everyone thought that he was dead. She'd been told that Moses was an Israelite who had been adopted into the palace as a young child and that when he was forty years old he killed an Egyptian who was beating a helpless Hebrew man. He had then fled into the desert. No one had heard from him since.

"What about the lost prince?" Father asked.

"He's come back!" Amasai exclaimed. "He's now an old man, nearly eighty years of age. He's come back demanding the Israelites' freedom, saying that Yahweh met him in the Midian desert and commanded him to lead the Israelites out of Egypt."

"What does that have to do with us working twice as hard as we do now?" Mother interrupted.

"The pharaoh was infuriated by Moses' request for freedom. He was so mad that he immediately said that we have to collect our own straw to make bricks. The Egyptians are not going to supply us with straw anymore. Not only that but we still have to produce the same amount of bricks, or more bricks, than we did before. The pharaoh was obviously in a rage. I'm surprised he didn't order Moses to be executed right then and there."

"Moses should've known no good would've come out of a confrontation with Pharaoh," Mother snapped. "What right does he have to come back here and get us all into trouble?"

Amasai shrugged, still scowling. "None of the elders are pleased. He's supposed to come and meet with us today along with his brother, Aaron. It seems that Yahweh has given them some form of divine power. But enough about that. We must get to work. Today, all our group is scouring the land for straw. Our ten families alone need to bring in one hundred bushels of straw. Hopefully that will last us until next week." Amasai exhaled, slowly.

"One hundred bushels?" Father said in shock.

"Yes, I know, but that's how many we need to supply us all week. Everyone needs to be out working today, including the young boys. Mariel, you are excused to continue weaving cloth. Eitan, you're going to be at the mixing pits. The rest of you, hurry up and find all the straw you can."

A stunned silence rested on the family as Amasai hurried on to the next hut. Everyone feverishly ran around gathering water and food for the day. Then they all ran to the marshlands, sickles in hand, ready to cut the thick grass and wild wheat that grew there. Jarah, Tirzah and Shayna worked as a team. But gathering sixty pounds of straw to make a full bushel was no easy task. Once they packed the straw together into tight bundles they tied them together with strips of cloth. Jarah hoisted the bushel to her back and, stooping over with the weight, she walked as fast as she could towards the marketplace where the straw was to be delivered. It was more than a mile walk just to get there.

Jarah's feet beat out a sad rhythm on the dirt street. Many other children and adults walked along next to her. Almost no one spoke. The weight they were carrying, and the weight of knowing what would happen to them at the end of the day if they didn't work their hardest, pushed them onwards in a type of frenzied despair. Jarah lowered her head against the sun's blinding rays, focusing on the ground in front of her. Her eyes misted with tears. She didn't want to go on. She didn't think she could go on. But she knew she had no choice. Swallowing the lump in her throat, Jarah pushed herself to go faster. It was still early morning. Maybe, just maybe, they could finish their work in time.

א

"Eight," Jarah grunted, strapping another bushel to her back. Her feet were sore. Her shoulders were throbbing.

"Hurry," Shayna panted. Her hands were bleeding and she was drenched in sweat and covered in dirt. "There's only one hour 'til sundown. Keep working."

Jarah nodded and turned once again onto the road.

Only one more hour. In a way it was a relief to know that work was almost over. But did they have enough straw? Had the other families done their job? Jarah knew she probably only had time for one more bushel, at best.

I can do this, I can do this, she kept telling herself. She urged herself to go even faster. Every movement she made seemed to drain more energy from her body, but she couldn't stop. Tears of absolute exhaustion clouded Jarah's vision. Her foot hit a stone. Jarah's ankle twisted and she fell to the ground with a low cry. Jarah could no longer keep her tears back. She sobbed in pain and anguish.

"Jarah!"

Jarah looked up and through her tears saw her best friend, Amissa, running towards her with a bushel of straw tied to her back. A voice next to her said, "Here, let's help you up." It was Amissa's fourteen-year-old brother, Ezra. Ezra and Amissa pulled Jarah to her feet.

"Thank you," Jarah murmured, choking back her sobs.

Amissa grabbed her hand and squeezed it. She looked so pale and tired. "Come on, let's walk together." Jarah could only nod back.

The three friends walked quickly towards the market. Jarah was limping a little. Her foot felt like it was swelling. But being in the presence of her friends helped her and encouraged her to keep going. Everyone was too tired to say anything, but every time Jarah slipped or moaned a little Amissa squeezed her hand and Ezra gave her his signature teasing grin. Even his dark eyes seemed to be smiling.

How can he be so happy? Jarah asked herself. *He looks just as tired and worn out as me and Amissa.*

"Jarah, did you go to the palace last night?" Amissa questioned, finally breaking the silence.

"Yes," Jarah muttered, shifting the weight on her back. "I saw Ada. Your sister told me, 'Tell them I'm fine, and that I'm seeing Yahweh at work in Egypt at last. They—and you—will see what I mean soon enough.'"

"Hmm… She must've been in the throne room when Moses was there," Ezra mused.

"Well, if Yahweh caused all this extra work, I don't know if I want anything to do with Him," Amissa grumbled angrily, kicking at some straw on the road.

Ezra turned his dark eyes to his sister and glared at her. "Amissa, I know you don't mean that. This isn't Yahweh's fault. It's the pharaoh's. Besides, maybe Ada's referring to something else."

Amissa looked down at her toes, looking sad and forlorn. "No, I guess I didn't really mean that. I'm sorry."

Jarah shook her head and grimaced as she put weight on her swollen foot. *Amissa may be sorry for what she said, but I think the same thing. If Yahweh caused this, I don't know if I want to have anything to do with Him, or Moses.* Jarah felt anger rising up in her chest. *How could Moses do this to us?* she wailed inwardly. She didn't know how she was supposed to make it through this day, let alone tomorrow. *Someone, anyone, please,* she cried, *please deliver us!*

ב

"Jarah," a voice hissed.

"Huh? What?" Jarah slowly rolled over and forced her eyes to open. Everything was blurry. Her eyelids were heavy. She felt so tired, and she hurt all over.

"Get up." It was her mother, shaking her arm. "It's breakfast time."

Jarah groaned and made herself get up. She staggered around the hut doing chores in a daze. She felt stupid and dumb with exhaustion. Her ankle was still sore. For two days their workload had been doubled. The hard work that they had all had to do—particularly the men—had left its mark on all of the Israelites. And still they hadn't met their daily quota of bricks for the last two days.

The other members of the family came in from doing chores and praying one by one. This morning they didn't all eat together. They just rushed through the meal and started to clean up. Jarah was bent over the washbowl when a shadow darkened the doorway. She spun around to see Amasai leaning heavily against the doorpost. Jarah almost screamed. His back was covered with blood. He had been whipped.

"Amasai!" Father and Eitan both leapt to their feet and ran to Amasai. They supported him, one on either side, and helped him sit down on a chair. Amasai let out a weak sigh and gratefully drank the water that Father offered him.

"I'll be all right in a moment," he said breathily. "I just can't walk much. But the pain will wear off soon, and I must go on." Amasai groaned and gingerly moved to a different position.

"What happened?" Father questioned.

Amasai slowly shook his head. "We didn't make the amount of bricks we need to yesterday or the day before. Almost all of the foremen didn't get their people to complete the extra work. It's just too much. But Pharaoh wouldn't listen. He ordered most of us to be whipped last night and sent us home in the dark in our disgrace. He didn't even send anyone with us to help us back to our dwellings. And that's when we saw that troublemaker—Moses." Amasai spat out the name. "He apologized for all that has happened to us but said that Yahweh still wants him here. Almost all of the elders and foremen wish the demon was back in the accursed desert." There was a moment of silence as Amasai finished his water and then rose to his feet.

"Everyone must work very hard today. If we don't make our quota, not only will I be whipped again but some of you might be whipped, too." He looked right in Jarah's eyes. He looked angry, but also very worried. Jarah's heart was pounding. She felt as if a huge weight was resting on her shoulders.

If I don't work my hardest, everyone will be punished. It'll be all my fault. Jarah gulped.

"Asher and Eitan, the pharaoh has ordered a new temple to be erected on the other side of the Nile. Go down to the dock. There will be boats to help you and the other Israelites get across. Lemuel, you'll be gathering clay for bricks, as usual. Shayna, we'll need help down at the sand pit repairing and making baskets and carrying sand. Jarah and Tirzah, you'll be beating out the papyrus to make scrolls again. We'll have to go to a different part of the Nile, though. We exhausted the supply of reeds in this part of Goshen. If you two will go join Ezra and Amissa I'll be back in a couple of moments to bring you up to Rameses. Be quick, all of you. And if anyone finishes their work early, go get some more straw. I'm afraid we're going to run out before next week." With a weary sigh, Amasai walked slowly and carefully out of the house.

Jarah and Tirzah quickly washed up and drank some water. They were the first ones outside. They ran over to Amissa's house next door. Amissa was already outside, waiting. She looked tired and white with dark circles under her blue eyes.

"Where's Ezra?" Jarah questioned.

"He'll be right here. He had to feed the animals," Amissa said, quietly. She appeared to be thinking about something.

"What's the matter?" Jarah prodded.

"Oh, I was just thinking about what Father said. He just came back from a meeting with the elders. I was just thinking about the amazing sign Aaron and Moses performed before the pharaoh last night."

"What amazing sign?" Jarah asked.

"You didn't hear about that?" Amissa's eyes widened. "To show Yahweh's power, Aaron turned his staff into a snake. The magicians turned their sticks into snakes, too, but it sounds like they used a fake magic. Anyways, Aaron's snake ate up the magicians' snakes. But the pharaoh was mad and sent Moses away."

"That's… that's amazing. A miracle!" Jarah gasped. "But—" She stopped and bit her lip.

"But what?" Amissa pressed.

"I'm not doubting that they had Yahweh's power, but… what good did it do? Work is still just as hard. Pharaoh's still making us get our own straw. Why did Yahweh make our work harder?" Jarah was trying hard to not be angry, but it wasn't working. She could tell that her face was flushed and her chest felt constricted, almost like she wanted to scream and yell. The weight of the responsibility on her shoulders and her wrath at Moses made her feel depressed and irritated.

Amissa looked down at her toes. "I don't know," she whispered softly. "I was just thinking the same thing."

Amasai came up to them, panting and grimacing with pain. He was taking slow, agonizing steps. "Sorry to keep you girls waiting. I had to give out the extra orders. Where's Ezra? We need to go."

"I'm here." Ezra dashed out from behind the house breathing hard, his golden-brown hair blowing in the wind. "Sorry," he said, coming up to Amasai. "I'm ready."

"Let's go." Amasai started off down the dusty street, moving as quickly as his wounds would allow him to go. Jarah kept her eyes down on the ground, trying not to look at Amasai's bloody back. She tried to think about where they would be working and getting her job done as fast as possible.

Ezra came up next to her. "You ready to work hard?" he asked, sending her his signature teasing grin. But Jarah didn't feel like smiling back.

"How can you be happy?" she asked, almost accusingly. "We still have twice the amount of work to do. What's there to be happy about?" It was all she could do to control her temper and keep from yelling at Ezra. She knew it wasn't his fault, but right now she didn't feel like acting happy.

"Well, if I wasn't happy, I'd be angry like you," Ezra teased. Jarah had to smile a little at that. "Besides, we don't have to make or move bricks. Our work won't be too much harder. Just longer. And you can't help but be a little excited that someone stood up to Pharaoh and didn't get killed for it. Yahweh's with Moses, and with Aaron. Something good is going to come out of this."

"How can you be so sure?" Jarah felt more like moping than celebrating.

Ezra shrugged. "I don't know. I just think Yahweh's going to do something big for us. He said someday we'd go to the Promised Land. And this is the first leader He's ever brought to us. Now let's hurry and catch up to Amasai."

Amasai led them to a section of the Nile that was south of the city of Rameses, but pretty close to the palace. Jarah could see Egyptian soldiers standing guard on top of a sand dune several hundred yards away.

"Get to work," Amasai urged. "Just stay around here. We don't want to get too close to the palace. Those guards would report us for sure." Amasai went over to an Egyptian overseer who stood several yards away on the bank of the Nile, watching the Israelites who were already at work. Ezra darted off to join the other men and boys who were pulling reeds from the water. Jarah, Amissa, and Tirzah joined a group of young women and girls who were laying out the papyrus reeds and beating them with mallets. Everyone worked quickly and quietly. They weren't allowed to talk much. The overseers thought that talk slowed them down. Jarah remembered a time when she was beaten for talking. She would never forget the nauseating pain of the whip's blows.

While they worked the heat increased and it soon became unbearable. Jarah's back felt like it was on fire.

At least I get to sit down, she thought, *though I wish there was some shade.* Jarah looked at the men who were pulling reeds. She felt so sorry for them. She could tell from the stains on the sand that some of their feet were beginning to bleed from stepping on the sharp reeds. Jarah quickly looked back at her work.

The three girls worked diligently and didn't stop to even wipe their hair from their faces, for the overseer working on this part of the Nile was watching them with eagle eyes. Jarah often felt the overseer's glare resting on her. It made her very nervous. He was looking at her with evil intent in his eyes. Hardly daring to move her eyes from the wooden mallet in her hand, Jarah worked so hard that her arms ached and trembled from the exertion. She was practically holding her breath, trying to work hard to gain the man's favor and not get whipped.

Finally the overseer moved on to another group of workers picking the papyrus reeds. Jarah shuddered and wished desperately that Ezra was around. Not only was he fun to work with but she would have loved his protective presence right about now. From the way the overseer was acting, she was worried that the he was going to beat her. She saw Ezra in the distance, dropping another bundle of reeds into the ever-growing pile by the street. The overseer was just beginning to beat an old man with a whip. Jarah hated the sound of the blood-curdling yells and the crack of the whip. And from the dark look on Ezra's face she could tell that he hated them, too. But Amissa frantically mouthed to Ezra, "Don't try anything," and Ezra slowly walked away, looking like he would have rather started a fight with the Egyptian for his unjustness instead of going back to work.

No matter how hard Jarah tried to focus on her work she kept thinking about Moses' plea and the pharaoh's injustice. She wondered if Ezra was right about Moses being their deliverer. But she couldn't entertain that thought for long. Every time she thought about Moses she got a little angrier. She couldn't help but be upset that he was the cause of more work.

Suddenly she heard laughter. Jarah looked up. In the distance she saw a covered, richly painted flat boat being poled along through the water. From the ornate wigs and the glint of gold, Jarah knew that a royal party was enjoying a morning ride on the Nile River. She saw what looked like a throne on the boat, and Jarah realized that the pharaoh was probably on board. It looked like they were having so much fun. Jarah envied their life of ease and began to feel even worse about the hardship she was enduring.

It's just not fair, she fumed. *We're people, too. We deserve a rest. We deserve to live like they live.*

A shout interrupted her thoughts. "It's Moses!"

Jarah brushed the damp hair away from her forehead and looked down the dirt road. Two men were coming their way. Through the haze of sand and heat, they came closer and closer. Jarah squinted her eyes and stared. The man on the right was the shorter and stouter of the two with a gray beard and a long walking stick. She recognized him as Aaron, one of the leading Levites in Goshen.

To the left, however, was quite a different man. He was tall, broad, and looked surprisingly strong for being an elderly man. He held a long staff and walked with determination and fearlessness. He carried himself like royalty. Jarah instantly knew who he was. He was Moses. Jarah felt anger seething inside of her. Here was the man who was causing all their extra trouble. What was he doing here? Was he coming to gloat over their weakness?

He better not come near me, Jarah thought, clamping her jaw shut to keep from yelling at him. *I don't want anything to do with him. He needs to go back to the desert where he belongs.*

Aaron and Moses were moving away from them now, up and over the sand dune and towards the Nile River. They were heading towards the pharaoh's boat. Jarah drew in her breath. She saw the soldiers who were guarding the palace in the distance exchange looks and appear a little uneasy.

They must be very brave, or very dumb. No one approaches Pharaoh without his permission on pain of death.

Jarah saw Aaron raise his staff. She faintly heard him yelling in a clear voice, "Pharaoh! The Lord, the God of the Hebrews, sent me to you saying, 'Let My people go, that they may serve Me in the wilderness.' Now behold, you have not listened to the voice of the Lord but have hardened your heart. Thus says the Lord, 'By this you will know that I am the Lord.' See, I will strike the water that is in the Nile with my staff, and it shall become blood, and all the fish that are in the Nile will die and the water will smell foul, and the Egyptians will have a hard time finding any water that is not turned to blood."

Everyone who was working around Jarah was frozen as they watched the two men and the boat that was drawing near to them. Jarah barely made out the form of Pharaoh standing at the side of the boat in open-mouthed rage and astonishment. Jarah heard him shout, "Seize them!"

The Egyptians who were poling the boat instantly altered their course for the shore. Pharaoh's bodyguards on board the float drew their swords. Jarah turned to look at Moses and Aaron. She expected them to run for their lives. But the men just stood there. Jarah's jaw dropped open.

They're going to get killed. They're being openly defiant. They're being really brave, but still, this is only going to bring more trouble to us, and to them!

Aaron now took a step forward. He raised his staff in the air and stretched it out over the Nile River. Unexpectedly, the surface of the water grew darker, and darker, and even darker until the muddy water of the Nile turned into a bright red! The Israelites jumped back from the river in horror, screaming. A wave of bright red water lapped up the bank, almost touching Jarah's feet. She shrieked and scrambled up the bank. Tirzah grabbed her and clung to her arm.

"What is it?" she cried.

Jarah turned to look at Aaron and Moses. Aaron was putting his staff down and nodding at Moses. Jarah heard high pitched cries and saw that the royal party on the boat was panicking, running around and screaming. The boat was pitching to and fro and one of the men working the poles fell into the water. He surfaced, yelling and shouting about blood.

"The water is *blood*?" Tirzah screamed.

Jarah shook her head. She was stunned and amazed. The water had actually turned into blood.

The panic on the river bank and the boat slowly died down. The shock and wonder of what had just happened ended in a silent awe that spread rapidly over the people on the river. Everyone's eyes fixed on the pharaoh who stood at the end of the float, staring in bewilderment at the water. His eyes fixed on Moses and Aaron, still standing fearlessly on the bank, surveying the scene.

The pharaoh finally gestured to his bargemen. "Go back. Back to the palace. Now! Go summon my magicians." The men polling the boat instantly obeyed. The pharaoh looked over his shoulder and shouted, "You shall see, Moses. Our gods are greater than yours. You shall see whose is better by the time this is over!" The pharaoh sounded confident, but Jarah thought that she heard a waver in his voice.

Jarah looked at Moses and Aaron. Even though they were far away, Jarah saw that they looked very sad. Moses and Aaron turned towards the town and continued their walk. Jarah's eyes followed them. She was still amazed by what had happened.

There was a great hubbub among the Egyptians on the shore and most of the overseers fled from the scene. One of the overseers turned to them and called out, "You're free to go home," and then ran from the vicinity of the Nile after his fellow comrades.

The Israelites were still frozen in wonder. Slowly the crowd began to dissolve and moved in a mass back to their homes. Jarah, Amissa, and Tirzah still stood on the riverbank, gazing off into the distance.

"That was amazing," Amissa murmured.

"How did he do it, Jarah?" Tirzah breathed in awe.

Jarah just shrugged. She felt dazed. All she knew was that the most wonderful miracle had been performed here today. She had never, ever heard of such a display of power. Not even from the magicians.

Ezra came running up to them. "That was incredible. Incredible!" he exclaimed. "Amissa, we've got to go back and tell them. Yahweh's working through Moses, just like Father said." Ezra was beaming with delight and excitement as he grabbed his sister's hand. "Come on. Let's go!"

Everyone ran back to their homes. Jarah's mind was whirling.

Moses has Yahweh's power. I saw it. Maybe, just maybe, we'll be free!

TRIUMPHS AND TRIALS

Jarah and Tirzah darted through the dusty streets of Goshen, laughing from amazement and disbelief.

"Work's cancelled. Can you believe it?" Jarah asked.

"No. I don't think work's ever been cancelled before," Tirzah replied. She was grinning from ear to ear.

"Me neither. I can't wait to get home. We can do whatever we want today, Tirzah! We could play all day if we wanted. Or sleep. Or eat. Or—I don't know! It just feels so good."

"It's almost like we're free," Tirzah breathed.

"Free…" Jarah whispered. The word felt and sounded so good. She was tasting freedom. Maybe this was just the beginning. Maybe they really would be free very, very soon.

Jarah and Tirzah came running into the house, laughing and out of breath. Their mother looked up in shock and bewilderment, sending the girls into peals of laughter.

"What are you doing here?" Mother gasped out. "What's happened?"

"Work's cancelled, Mother," Jarah announced.

"What? How? Why?"

Jarah and Tirzah quickly told the story about Moses, Aaron, and the river turning into blood. As they concluded their story their mother's face turned white.

"Impossible," she said as if in a daze. She was looking at Jarah but it seemed like she wasn't even seeing her, as if she was looking through her.

"Mother? What's wrong? Aren't you excited? We don't have to work," Jarah cried out, practically jumping up and down in delight.

"Stop it, both of you!" Mother barked. Both of the girls stood perfectly still, scared and startled by their mother's response. Mother spun around on her stool to face them, eyes flashing. "Work isn't done. There are chores to do. More straw needs to be collected. And I can't stop working. I have almost twice the amount of linen to make this week for the queen. And that's not it. How could this Moses have done this? The Nile is sacred! It provides us with water all year long. Without it, we'll die!"

Jarah's heart was pounding. *I hadn't thought of that. There's no water. What'll we do?*

Tirzah quietly piped up, "But Mother, what do you mean, the Nile is sacred?"

"The Egyptians, I mean, *we*, worship the Nile as our source of provision. Something very serious must have happened with the Egyptian gods to let such a terrible thing happen. I can't believe it." Mother choked, as if about to cry, and then quickly spun back around on her stool and began speedily weaving cloth on her loom.

Jarah's excited, hopeful mood had been crushed by her mother's words. *Maybe... Maybe the Egyptians gods don't control the Nile like we thought. Maybe, just maybe, Yahweh is the true God. Moses and Aaron called on Yahweh's name. He answered them. I saw Him give Aaron the power. But could Yahweh want us to die of thirst? Surely He wouldn't do that. Or would he...?*

Jarah heard the sound of running feet and saw Shayna come in the door, gasping for air.

"Mother, do you know what happened?" Shayna began. But Mother quickly cut her off.

"Yes, yes. I know all about it. It's nothing to get excited about, girl. Something's wrong with the Egyptian gods, and that's not a cause for celebration. Be a good girl and come help me."

"But Mother, haven't you heard the stories? The men called on Yahweh, and—"

"Stop it! I don't want to hear about Yahweh. What, are you changing your beliefs, too?" Mother demanded.

Shayna paused and shifted her weight uncomfortably as her mother's angry hazel eyes bored into hers. She gulped and cleared her throat before responding, "No, Mother." She lifted up her chin, tossed her hair in a haughty fashion, and sat down next to Mother. Jarah rolled her eyes at Tirzah.

I wish Shayna would stop trying to act confident and own up to the fact that she's struggling just as much as I am with these things. She's not fooling me with her confident airs.

"Mother!" Eitan ran into the house. He looked concerned. "Oh good. You're here, Shayna. Lemuel needs help. He got whipped only once for spilling some clay, but the whip opened up an old wound. Father's bringing him back now."

Shayna nodded and darted out the back door to the garden to get some herbs.

"Mother, did you hear about the Nile?" Eitan continued.

"Yes, yes. Jarah and Tirzah were there and saw the whole thing. Now you can stop talking about it," Mother snapped, irritably.

Eitan turned to Jarah, his eyes glowing. "You saw the water turn into blood? What was it like?"

Jarah barely had time to tell Eitan the story when Father came in slowly, holding Lemuel's arm to stabilize him. He eased Lemuel onto a stool and that's when Jarah saw the blood staining his back. She gasped. Lemuel looked up at her and grinned, weakly. His face was so pale.

"I'll be all right. It's not as bad as it looks," he said with forced cheerfulness. Jarah nodded and tried to smile back. Shayna came back into the house with some herbs and hurried to the bag of scrap fabric to find a bandage.

"Jarah, Tirzah, you don't need to watch this," Mother said. "Go out and get your brothers. You should all bring more straw to the market."

"Yes, Mother," the girls responded.

As they headed towards the garden where the little boys were, Jarah had a sinking feeling in her chest.

I thought today was going to be so good. But now Lemuel's hurt, Mother's in a terrible mood, we still need to collect straw, and there's no water. Or is there?

They had reached the garden which was on a sloping green hill. In this area of Goshen there were many large creeks that kept the land green all year long. Jarah suddenly got an idea.

"Tirzah, stay here with the Raphael and Yanni. I'll be right back." She ran up the hill, hoping, praying that she would see what she wanted to see.

She was up the hill in a moment and was able to look out to where a large creek flowed through Goshen. She squealed in delight and shouted, "Tirzah, come look. The water here isn't blood! Come look!"

Tirzah and the boys ran up the hill. Tirzah drew in her breath. "How? How'd Yahweh do it?"

"I don't know. It's a miracle."

"Jarah? Are you all right?" Jarah looked back towards the house and saw her father standing at the back door.

"Father!" Jarah ran back down the hill followed by her siblings. "Our water isn't blood. We still have water. Yahweh protected our water!"

A broad grin spread across Father's face. "Well that's something to tell your mother now, isn't it?"

א

Jarah and Tirzah walked through the streets, balancing baskets of laundry on their heads. Once their mother heard that they actually had water she had insisted on several chores being done and the house being tidied up a bit. Father and Eitan took Raphael and Yanni to get more straw and Jarah and Tirzah volunteered to go wash clothes in the creek. They both loved being in the cool water. Though the day of freedom wasn't turning out exactly as Jarah had hoped, she found that she was humming a song of worship to Yahweh as she and Tirzah made their way through the crowded streets. Many other people were singing, too. Foreign sounds of happiness greeted Jarah's ears. She smelled the wonderful smells of bread baking and saw children playing and adults laughing and talking together. She hadn't seen the Israelites this happy in a long, long time.

"Maybe Yahweh really does listen," Jarah whispered to herself.

"What's that?" Tirzah asked.

"Oh, nothing," Jarah answered, shrugging.

Soon they were at the creek, setting down their baskets on the quiet bank. The soap they used was made out of the fat from their animals and the girls were soon ankle-deep in cool, rippling water, surrounded by soapy bubbles and wet clothes.

"Did you hear what Mother told Shayna as we were leaving?" Tirzah asked.

"No, what?" Jarah murmured, distractedly. She was thoroughly enjoying the peace and stillness.

"She said that she was going to measure us for new dresses today or tomorrow. I can't wait."

Jarah couldn't help but smile at her sister's excitement. She, too, had been wanting a new dress. Hers was very short, almost above her knees. It wasn't really considered modest by Hebrew standards. She wanted a beautiful, long, flowy dress of white linen.

"I wonder what our new dresses will look like," Jarah sighed dreamily, imagining herself as a servant in the palace, dressed in an exquisite new dress that swished as she walked.

"Probably not linen," Tirzah began, sulkily. "Linen's too expensive. Mother has some wool fabric left over. It's red with white and black stripes. Remember? That would make a pretty dress."

"Shalom Jarah. Shalom Tirzah," came a cheery voice from behind them. Jarah turned abruptly and saw Amissa coming towards them, also holding a half-filled basket with her family's dirty clothes. "Mind if I join you?" she asked in a jesting tone.

"No. Not one bit," Jarah replied, throwing a teasing look at her friend.

Amissa waded into the water with them and then said, "Ada might come back home tonight. It appears that some of the Egyptians were accusing her and some other Israelites of angering the gods. So the queen might send them back home for safety."

"Really?" Tirzah asked eagerly.

Amissa nodded, a smile spreading rapidly across her pretty face. "We hardly ever see her. She's the queen's personal attendant, you know. So we're very excited. It's been over six months since she was able to come home, though thanks to you and another Egyptian, Paki, we get lots of messages from her."

"Do you think she'll be safe?" Jarah asked. "No one's really going to hurt her, right?"

"Oh, she'll be fine if your brother has anything to do with it," Amissa giggled.

"What do you mean?" Jarah demanded.

"Well," Amissa's eyes darted to and fro and her eyes smiled as if she was revealing a great secret. "My father was talking to your father about Ada and how he hoped she'd be safe. Eitan looked really, really worried and asked if he could help in any way. You should've seen his face, Jarah." Amissa burst into laughter and made Jarah laugh, too. She could just picture her older brother looked very concerned about the beautiful young maid.

"Jarah?" Jarah spun around and saw Shayna a few yards away, holding a clay jar. "What do you think you're doing? It's not time to play around. We have work to do."

Jarah felt angry at her sister. She was working. What was wrong with talking and laughing while she worked? Jarah was about to yell out in anger but then she caught herself and silently prayed, *Dear Yahweh, please help me.* She somehow managed to look her sister squarely in the eye and reply, "Yes, Shayna. I know. I'm working now," and she turned back to her work, a smile of triumph on her lips.

I did it. I did it. I didn't yell at her. Jarah's heart jumped for joy. Yahweh was helping her. Maybe He was not only as powerful and mighty as Father said, but a loving God who really took an interest in each of His people.

ב

For the rest of the day Jarah's heart soared. She felt such a freedom that she had never experienced before. She felt so peaceful and happy. She was able to get away by herself and go out into the fields and sit and pray to Yahweh like she had never prayed before. Jarah began to think that maybe, just maybe, Yahweh cared about her. She wasn't sure if she trusted Him yet, but she wanted to.

In the evening, Shayna went to go and talk to Ada. But Ada had not been able to come home. Instead, she had sent a message through an Egyptian to her family.

"Ada's still at the palace, but she's safe," Shayna said. Jarah was satisfied to see a worried look cross momentarily over Eitan's face. "She sent a message, though, and she said all the Egyptians are very worried. They have absolutely no water," Shayna announced to the rest of the family with a smug smile. "They had to dig fresh wells to find some. The pharaoh doesn't seem too concerned but everyone else in the palace is very afraid. They've ordered a fast and the temples are filled with Egyptians making petitions to the gods."

"I wish I could go pray with them," Jarah heard her mother mumble under her breath. She looked up and realized that Father had heard her mother, too.

"Let's spend some time singing praises to Yahweh before we go to sleep tonight," Father said. He looked around the room, smiling at each of them. "I feel like I'm a part of a different family tonight. You all have been so happy and kind today. Thank you."

ג

The next morning, Jarah was astonished to find that when she woke up, the sun was already half-way up the sky.

How did I oversleep? she rebuked herself as she sprang from bed. But as she looked around, the only other one awake in their house was Eitan.

"What's happening, Eitan?" Jarah questioned in a whisper.

"The Nile is still blood, so work has been canceled for another day," Eitan said quietly, but with evident excitement. "Several overseers came to the elders of Israel last night to say that work was cancelled until they could find another main water source."

"That means we could have several more days of freedom, right?" Jarah asked, hopefully. She couldn't believe that they might not have to work for several more days. The Egyptians had never cancelled their work.

Eitan smiled and nodded. "Maybe, if Yahweh wills it."

Everyone woke up late that morning and chores were done in a slow, but yet productive way. It was early in the afternoon when Jarah got around to airing out the beds. Sounds drifted in to her from the open windows. Out front, Tirzah was trying to explain to Raphael and Yanni how important it was to take turns sharing the ball they played with. Father, Eitan, and Lemuel were fixing the wagon out back and were laughing and jesting. Their high spirits filled Jarah with hope. But then she heard an unwelcome sound—boisterous laughter. Jarah sighed and looked out the window. Shayna was standing in the shadow of the house across the street, flirting with Mayer and Zephon. Jarah's lips curled up in disgust as Shayna inched towards Mayer and took his arm, standing awfully close to him.

Shayna needs to stop that. She's going to get a bad reputation. And then it'll get passed down to Tirzah and me and—

Jarah's bitter thoughts were interrupted by her mother calling, "Jarah, come here. I need to get you measured for your new dress."

"Coming, Mother," Jarah responded, setting down the blanket she was folding and running over eagerly.

As her mother pulled out the string that she used for measuring, Jarah's eyes scanned the table cluttered with scraps of fabric. She saw a pile of pastel blue and purple linen on the far corner of the table and her face lit up with delight. *Please, please,* she begged inside, *let that linen be for me.*

Her mother continued to measure her, checking her height and how wide her waist was.

"What kind of dress is Tirzah getting?" Jarah asked.

"She's getting one out of the black wool," her mother replied, bluntly.

"Oh," Jarah whispered with a smile, knowing Tirzah would be happy. "What about Shayna?"

"She's getting one made out of that linen over there." Mother jerked her head towards the end of the table.

Jarah's heart sank as she shyly wondered aloud, "What about me?"

"I have some of that blue wool left over. It'll make you a suitable dress."

"Oh."

"Don't look so disappointed! You can't have everything you want and that linen will serve as a wedding and betrothal dress for Shayna. You won't need anything fancy for several years to come. And besides, I don't approve of girls wearing things that are too pretty. They will become conceited and will want to show off around young men," said Mother, matter-of-factly.

As if I will and Shayna won't. Jarah gritted her teeth bitterly. *Shayna flirts with boys already. Why, she's outside right now talking with Zephon and Mayer.* Jarah watched as Shayna walked arm-in arm-down the street with the two boys. Jarah angrily blinked back tears and looked at the medium blue wool. It was nice in its own way but much too homely for what Jarah had been wishing for. *Why must Shayna be Mother's favorite child?* Jarah's thoughts roared in her ears. *It's just not fair. Father doesn't have a favorite.*

"Don't be bitter, Jarah," a calm, quiet voice soothed. "Good things come to those who wait and trust in Me."

Jarah's eyes darted around the room. *Who is that? Where'd that strange voice come from?* No one else was around besides Mother. And it wasn't Mother's voice. It sounded almost like Father's voice, but deeper, and in some ways, more powerful.

"Do you trust Me, Jarah?"

There it was again. Jarah was positive she had heard it, even though it sounded far away and distant. But it also felt like it was there all at the same time. And it was so soft and gentle that it made her feel warm all over.

Who is it? Jarah wondered. Aloud she said, "Did you hear that, Mother?"

"Hear what?" her mother asked.

"Nothing." Jarah looked around. *Am I hearing things?*

"Jarah." The voice murmured her name again.

Yes? Jarah spoke silently.

"Do you know Me?"

N-no. I don't believe I do. Who are you?

"I am the God of your fathers, the God of Abraham, Isaac, and Jacob. I know your heart, my child, and it is devoted to Me. I promise I will never leave you, nor forsake you. Just trust in Me and I will give you rest."

The voice slowly faded away and was gone. Jarah stood as if rooted to the floor. Her mouth was wide open in astonishment. Yahweh had just talked to *her*. She knew it. The thought was so wonderful and so terrible at the same time that she didn't know what to do or how to respond.

"Jarah, did you hear me?" The vexed voice brought Jarah back to reality.

"What, Mother?" Jarah shook her head to clear her thoughts.

"Go pick some turnips and lentils. We need to get started on dinner," her mother commanded.

"Yes, Mother," Jarah replied meekly.

ז

The next morning, order was restored. Once the Egyptians discovered that the Irsaelites had plenty of pure water they quickly put them to work, hauling their water to the Egyptian city and construction sites. Thus the happy times were over for Jarah, her family, and all the other Israelites. Work was at once resumed in full swing, and it seemed even harder now that they had to haul water back and forth on top of supplying their own straw. And in a couple of days, the Nile resumed its natural color.

FROGS?

For a whole week they worked. Every night Jarah and the rest of her family members came home sore, dissatisfied, and irritable. Every day the sun seemed to get hotter and brighter. Every day Mother seemed more and more controlling and her family seemed to be separating again. The cold, foreboding look resting on Mother's and Shayna's faces became almost unbearable. Jarah avoided all contact with them as far as it was possible. Her father seemed to be getting weaker and weaker, and Jarah was constantly worried about him. From the looks exchanged between Eitan and Lemuel, Jarah could also tell they were also very concerned.

Then one morning, Father was too sore, weak, and sick to get out of bed.

"What are we going to do?" Jarah heard Lemuel ask Eitan.

"We'll just say he's sick and offer to take on his work as well as ours. It will be a long, hard day." Eitan sighed despondently. "But we have to do it."

There was a pause before Lemuel nodded his head and murmured, "Yes, I agree. We have to."

Shayna was kneeling by Father's side, attending to him. She stood up and told Eitan, "As far as I can tell, he doesn't have a fever or infection. I think it's simply fatigue. I'll try and get him to eat."

"Humph. Fatigue. He could get over fatigue if he wanted to," Mother mumbled, loud enough for everyone to hear. Father turned his head to the wall, but not before Jarah saw tears form in his eyes. Her father's sadness and her mother's harsh words hurt her heart.

Breakfast was eaten in a hurried silence. The table was cleared mechanically. Jarah was still cleaning off the dishes when Amasai came in.

"Let's get to work," Amasai commanded. "Asher, Eitan, and Lemuel, you'll be moving bricks to the new monument, and—"

"Amasai." Eitan stepped forward. "Father's not well. He can barely get out bed. I'm afraid Lemuel and I will have to take on his share of work for the day."

Amasai's eyes were wide. "But Eitan, that's almost impossible."

"I know, but we don't have a choice. Father can't go to work today." Eitan's voice was quiet and respectful, but also forceful.

Amasai sighed a little and shrugged. "You both are going to have to be prepared to stay into the night hours."

"Yes, we know," Eitan said.

"Very well," Amasai said, resignedly. Turning to Shayna he said, "Shayna, you have a very different assignment today. One of the cooks in the palace kitchen is sick. There's a big feast tonight to celebrate one of the Egyptian gods, and I was asked to find a pretty young Hebrew woman who can cook in the kitchen and help serve at the feast. I think you will be good for that task."

Jarah's jaw dropped. *Shayna gets to work in the palace?* Jarah felt envy flood over her like a wave of water, but she controlled herself as Amasai turned towards her.

"Jarah and Tirzah, you'll be working in the palace today, too, washing clothes. The Egyptians are overwhelmed with the amount of laundry they have to do before the feast tonight."

Frogs?

What? We get to work in the palace, too? Washing clothes? Jarah could feel a smile steal across her face. At last she could be in the palace.

"I'll be back in a few minutes to bring you girls to the palace. Oh, and do you have anything nicer to wear? They want whoever comes to the palace to be clean and well-dressed," Amasai said.

"Yes. I just made them new dresses recently," Mother replied coolly, though with evident pride.

"Good. Get ready quickly. I'll be back in a moment." Amasai left, followed closely by Eitan and Lemuel.

"Don't just stand there. Hurry up and get dressed," Mother yelled. Then she murmured to herself, "Praise be to Ra that I thought of making those dresses when I did. What an honor to have children working in the palace," and she scooped up Yanni, balanced him on her hip, and limped out of the house to finish cleaning up after breakfast.

Shayna practically flew to the chest where their new dresses were stored. Shoving them towards the girls she commanded, "Put them on fast. We may have time to braid and cover our hair if we hurry."

Shayna's always so concerned about her outward appearance. Jarah looked at her sister with an annoyed expression, but Shayna didn't notice. She was too busy putting on her linen dress and smoothing out the intricate folds. *But that dress is lovely on her,* Jarah admitted to herself. She watched as Shayna pulled back the top layer of her hair and tied it with a frayed strand of silver cording, revealing some delicate, looping ringlets underneath. She also pulled the shawl that matched the dress around and over her head, covering it. She quickly spun Tirzah around, pulled out some black wool and tied it like a headband.

"Jarah, you're just standing there staring. Get on your dress and comb your hair. It's so tangled. I'll fix it as soon as I'm done with Tirzah."

Jarah slid into her dress and then grabbed the broken bone comb from the table where Shayna had just laid it. Vainly she attempted to push it through her gnarly hair. But before she had even begun getting the tangles out of it, Jarah felt Shayna running her fingers through her hair.

"Ouch," Jarah yelled.

"Hold still," Shayna scolded, pulling back all of Jarah's hair into a long, thick braid.

The girls were just tying on their leather sandals when Amasai came back into the house. He gave them an approving nod and then commanded, "Come with me." The girls followed him without a word, trying hard to keep up with his long, quick strides.

Amasai led them to the edge of Rameses. Here, an Egyptian guard was standing.

"These are the girls that are to go to the palace today," Amasai explained to the man. The Egyptian's sharp eyes peered at them for a long moment before he grunted and nodded his head in approval.

"They'll do. Come." Motioning to the girls, the man turned and started down a long alleyway and into the depths of the city. The girls ran after him. Jarah was relieved that they could walk through the streets in safety. However, all of the shrines raised to the gods and sacred objects made Jarah shudder as she saw their hideous shapes.

As they turned a bend in the road, Jarah saw the Egyptian girl and her little brother again. The boy was playing in the street with a ball of cloth and some sticks. The girl was just poking her head out of the front door.

"Bes, come inside. It's time for breakfast," she said, cheerily.

"Coming Acenith!" Bes said, with an obvious lisp. As he reached out to grab his ball, he saw Jarah. Jarah smiled at him. The boy's face lit up in a grin and he ran to Acenith shouting, "Wook! It's that girl!"

Acenith looked very surprised to see Jarah walking behind an Egyptian guard and dressed in nice clothes. Jarah nodded her head in respect, smiling at her. Acenith looked her in the eyes, ducked her head slightly, and then grasped Bes's arm and dragged him inside, saying, "We don't need to concern ourselves with her. I already told you that."

"Is she going to the pawace?" Bes asked, looking at Jarah over his shoulder.

"I don't know and I don't care," Acenith nearly shouted in rage, slamming the door.

Something in Acenith's tone struck Jarah. The girl sounded almost sad. Bitter, maybe? Was she lonely? Where were her parents? Jarah

Frogs?

had seen a sorrowful, almost empty look in Acenith's eyes this time. Maybe, did she want a friend? Jarah shook her head.

You're being ridiculous. Why would she want to be friends with you?

Finally, the guard led them up to the door which opened to the outer courtyard into which Jarah had gone so many times. A guard stood before the door, as always. But he didn't say anything or seem to even take notice of them, seeing another Egyptian leading them.

"Go on in through the courtyard. Someone will give you instructions for the day," the guard said gruffly before disappearing down a side street. Shayna stepped forward and opened the door, trying to look confident. The girls filed in, cautiously.

There was not a sound in the garden except for the rippling fountain in its center and the soft thud of their sandaled feet on the marble floor. Huge, exotic plants surrounded the high garden walls and perfumed the air, and many couches were laid out, possibly for a party. They reached the large door and Shayna knocked on it. It almost immediately opened. Standing in the doorway was Ada, looking just as lovely as usual with her genuine, welcoming smile.

"Shalom. I'm so glad to see you. Come in. I'm sure you will enjoy seeing the inside of the palace."

Jarah found herself in a large kitchen with white-washed brick walls. Clay pots lined every shelf and everything was spotless from the tile floors to the ceiling. There were several brick ovens and a pantry where wild fowl were hanging from the ceiling. A cook was at this moment mincing onions and the smell of the savory dish that she was making was overpowering. Jarah's stomach growled, reminding her that she had eaten very little that morning.

"Shayna, this is Tehara, the main cook for the queen. One of her assistants, as you probably know, is sick today, and you'll be helping her." Tehara glanced up at Shayna with a slight smile and nodded, but her eyes quickly fell back down to her work. Aside to Shayna, Ada whispered, "She's an older lady and she can be quite strict at times. Just obey her wishes and try not to talk too much. I'm sure you'll get along fine." Ada moved to Jarah and Tirzah and whispered, "Come with me." Ada opened the low kitchen door directly to their left and they stepped out into a luxuriant covered courtyard.

It was wide and open, with marble floors and huge, thick pillars supporting the stone roof. Everything was immaculate with rich rugs, settees, and couches in arrangements about the grand courtyard. Two black cats sat on one of these, licking their paws with an air of importance and indolence. In the center of the hall, a large fountain bubbled. The roof directly above the fountain was open to the light and rain. The strange scent of incense and exotic flowers filled the air. The whole front side of the courtyard was open, except for the decorative pillars that supported the roof. Between the pillars there were some stairs leading down to a shallow area in the Nile River. The view of the sand dunes in the distance and the Nile River, winding like a snake through the sand, was impressive.

"Over this way," Ada beckoned them. At the top of the stairs leading down to the Nile there were many baskets, filled to the brim with white linen. "All of these need to be washed. We wash the clothes in the Nile and then lay them on the steps to dry. Once they are dry you should fold them and put them back in the baskets. Be very neat and precise. The queen is very orderly and does not like things wrinkled or out of place. There's a bar of soap in all of the baskets. If you run out of soap just ask Tehara where to find some. And if you see any soldiers don't be alarmed. They patrol this area quite frequently. Just don't go exploring or stray from your tasks and they won't mind you. Now, I must go attend to the queen. She needs her morning bath and she doesn't like to be kept waiting." And Ada floated up a flight of stairs at the far end of the hall.

"Now what?" Tirzah whispered in a barely audible voice.

"We wash clothes," Jarah replied with a confident manner, though her limbs were trembling. She decided it would be best not to tell Tirzah that she, too, was nervous. She picked up a light woven basket and went down the stairs. She entered the water, warily looking out for crocodiles. Tirzah joined her and they worked in relative silence. Jarah's heart was thumping in her chest as she thought about hundreds of people who could be looking at them right now from the black windows of the palace.

"It's so quiet," Tirzah murmured. "I think I only saw three or four servant girls."

Frogs?

"Yes," Jarah said softly. "Everything looks perfect. But haven't you noticed the way it feels?" Tirzah's eyes were wide with fear and she shook her head. "It feels dark, doesn't it? Like… like there's something oppressive here. It feels like something's weighing down on me. Can you feel it?"

"Yes, a little," Tirzah said, shivering.

"I wonder if it has something to do with the Egyptian gods," Jarah said, more to herself than to Tirzah. Then she chuckled a little.

"What?" Tirzah asked.

"I've been wanting to be in the palace for so long. But now that I'm here, I can't wait to leave," Jarah said.

Tirzah didn't say anything for a minute. She finally answered in a shaky voice, "Me too."

Both of the girls had just finished two baskets of clothes and laid them out to dry when Tirzah grabbed Jarah's arm and screamed.

"Jarah! What's that?" Tirzah was screaming and pointing wildly towards the river. Jarah looked and felt like screaming herself. The Nile River was bubbling. It was churning and swirling.

"What is it?" Tirzah shrieked, jumping out of the water.

"I—I don't know." Jarah tried to be calm, but her voice was quivering. She climbed out onto the steps next to Tirzah, hoping it wasn't a bunch of crocodiles.

Suddenly the swirling, bubbling water started rising. It was coming up the stairs.

"Run!" Jarah cried. She and Tirzah grabbed the baskets of clothes and bolted to the top of the stairs. They turned around, eyes wide.

"Is it a flood?" Tirzah gasped.

Before Jarah could answer, something, a great black something, was leaping out of the churning water, spreading as far as she could see down both banks of the Nile! Tirzah screamed again. Jarah's heart was pounding in her ears. She could hear the palace coming alive behind her with cries and shrieks of terror. Soldiers were all around Tirzah and Jarah now, yelling and questioning. Jarah grabbed Tirzah and ran behind a pillar, shielding them from the soldiers. The black mass kept advancing. But as it advanced, Jarah realized that it wasn't one thing but a lot of the same thing. It was jumping, hopping towards them. She suddenly realized that they were frogs.

"Frogs," she exclaimed.

"Frogs?" Tirzah gasped.

The black thing was a mass of huge frogs. They were everywhere. They hopped right into the palace. The soldiers were shouting and trying to push the frogs back. Maids and servants were running around chaotically. A frog hopped on Jarah's leg. She tried to shake it off of her leg, but it wouldn't let go. Jarah grabbed it and threw it. The frogs were bigger than her hand. They were jumping on Tirzah now. She was going frantic, panicking.

I've got to get Tirzah out of here. With determination, Jarah grabbed Tirzah's hand.

"Let's go," she cried above the hubbub of croaking frogs and terrified people. She pulled Tirzah out from the shelter of the pillar and dashed across the courtyard. Frogs were everywhere. She couldn't move without stepping on one. They were jumping on everything, tearing the curtains and knocking over pots and plants. Jarah saw an idol on a shelf get knocked over, fall to the floor, and shatter. Jarah kept running into petrified maids, angry soldiers, and more and more frogs. The maids were shrieking and crying. Jarah quickly became lost in the crowd of Egyptians. She couldn't find her way through the chaos.

"Jarah, what do we do?" Tirzah wailed.

Jarah felt like wailing herself. She didn't know how to get them out of this. What could she do? Just then, she felt a gentle hand grab her arm. She spun around and found herself face to face with a pale Ada.

"Come with me," she gasped. Jarah and Tirzah gladly obeyed. Ada quickly weaved in and out of the crowd and then shoved both of the girls out of a door onto a portico. She slammed the door behind her. Jarah was relieved to be in the open air but she saw that the frogs were taking over the city. Absolute terror and horror was reigning.

"You girls must leave immediately," Ada cried, shepherding the girls towards a small gate in the wall. "Some of the Egyptians who hate the Hebrews will remember that you were here today. They might think you cast a magic spell that caused all this. You must go, now." Ada pulled open the gate.

Frogs?

"What about you and Shayna?" Jarah asked.

"I'll be fine. The queen will keep me from danger. But she doesn't know you, and since you're new in the palace you would be the first ones suspected of mischief. Now go! I'll send Shayna right after you." Ada pushed them out the gate and quickly closed it behind them.

"Come on," Jarah said, grabbing Tirzah's hand again.

The girls ran through the Egyptian streets which were filled with frogs and distressed people. The Egyptians were closing their doors and windows, but the frogs were still hopping inside. Some little children who began to chase the frogs were jerked inside by their mothers. Horses were whinnying, cows were lowing. Jarah and Tirzah made their way as fast as they could through the streets. They were both covered in slime and kept stepping on frogs. Jarah gasped as she realized that even more frogs were appearing every second, crawling out of gutters and mud puddles!

Suddenly, amidst all the other sounds, Jarah heard an almost frantic voice.

"Bes? Bes! Where are you?"

Jarah turned and saw Acenith across the street, searching in her courtyard for her little brother. Was he missing in this confusion?

That's when Jarah heard it. A happy laugh. She saw Bes sitting in the middle of the street, a huge frog in his chubby hands.

"Cenith, look," he cried in pure delight.

But Acenith wasn't delighted. She was petrified. She was so scared she couldn't move. And Jarah saw why. A chariot was charging down the street—right towards Bes. The frightened horse was out of control and the rider was panicking, trying to pull the horse in. Acenith finally forced herself to sprint into action but Jarah knew that she wouldn't get to her brother in time. She was even farther away than Jarah was. Jarah instantly knew what she had to do.

"Stay here," Jarah shouted to Tirzah. She bolted towards Bes.

"Jarah, don't!" Tirzah cried out in alarm.

But Jarah didn't turn back. Her heart was pounding in her ears as she saw the chariot coming closer and closer by the second. Bes had just noticed it, but as he jumped up to move out of the way he slipped on another frog. He screamed as he fell back on the street. Jarah could see the horse closing in. Frantically she put on a final burst of speed, grabbed Bes, and rolled. She heard an ear-piercing shriek along with the roar and clatter of the chariot's wheels in her ears and the *squish* of frogs being smashed. Then the chariot was gone. Jarah's heart felt like it was jumping up and down inside of her chest. She sat up and looked at Bes, hoping, praying he was all right. The boy's eyes were glued to hers. His lip was quivering and tears spilled down his cheeks. Frogs were jumping all over them and clawing them.

"Bes!" Acenith was right next to Jarah now. She flung her arms around Bes and pulled him into a tight embrace.

"I alwight, Cenith. I alwight," the little boy said, quietly, throwing his chubby hands around his sister's neck.

Jarah exhaled deeply, relief and joy washing over her. She quickly jumped up and started towards Tirzah, avoiding as many frogs as she could. Tirzah stood as if rooted to the dirt road. Her face was as white as a sheet. Jarah had to dodge frogs and frantic chickens and ducks in order to reach her sister.

"It's all right," Jarah said, gently grabbing Tirzah's hand. She was relieved that she was able to keep her voice from shaking. Her knees were still knocking together and she could tell that her face was as pale as Tirzah's. "Come on. We've got to get back," Jarah said, forcing a smile. Tirzah simply nodded. They started to walk quickly down the road when Jarah heard a shout.

"Wait!"

Spinning around, Jarah saw Acenith running towards them. She still held Bes close to her breast and tears were flowing down her olive-colored cheeks.

"Yes, young lady?" Jarah asked hesitantly, curtsying slightly.

Acenith stopped in front of them. She was looking down at her toes as if embarrassed. She cleared her throat and said softly, "I—I have to thank you. Bes is my only sibling and my only friend in the whole world. And if he had been killed..." The girl's lower lip was trembling uncontrollably and she took a moment to regain her composure before finishing. "If he'd been killed I don't know what Father would've done. I would've never been able to forgive myself." She paused and wiped away a tear. "Thank you. Thank you so much."

Frogs?

"You're welcome, my lady," Jarah gracefully lowered her head in reverence, blushing slightly from the praise and thanks.

"And please," Acenith said rather abruptly, her intense black eyes suddenly meeting Jarah's, "will you—forgive me? For—for being, so mean to you." She started sobbing again. "You seem like a nice girl, and obviously you're very brave. I just, I mean, since you're a Hebrew... Well, I shouldn't have treated you like—like dirt. I'm sorry. Can you ever forgive me?"

Jarah smiled as she gazed into Acenith's dark, sad eyes. "Of course, my lady."

A beautiful, rosy smile broke out over Acenith's face. "Thank you, but you don't have to call me that. Please, just call me Acenith."

"Yes, Acenith," Jarah said, grinning still more.

"What's your name?" Acenith asked.

"I'm Jarah."

"Well then, thank you, Jarah, for saving Bes. I will never, ever forget you." There was a slight pause as the two girls looked at each other.

"You'd better go," Acenith said at length as a frog leaped on her arm. She swatted it away.

"Yes. Good-bye, Acenith." Jarah nodded her head slightly, took Tirzah's hand, and ran back towards Goshen.

"Here—here's the street," Jarah shouted to Tirzah over the screams of an Egyptian servant girl as she tried to get away from the frogs. Jarah turned quickly and pulled Tirzah down the road.

As soon as they entered Goshen the girls stopped, almost in mid-step.

"Where are all the frogs?" Tirzah asked quietly, as if by asking the question the frogs would suddenly appear.

"I... I don't know." Jarah looked around. There were a few of the big frogs here, but not nearly as many as there had been in Rameses.

"Yahweh must be protecting us somehow," Jarah said. "I don't know how, but there are practically no frogs here."

The girls just stood, staring. Only a few yards behind them the mass of frogs was so thick that the frogs were on top of each other. In front of them, there were almost no frogs at all.

"Can we go home now?" Tirzah asked, softly. It sounded like she was about to cry.

Jarah nodded and put her arm around her sister. "Yes," she said, letting out a shaky breath. "We can go home."

Suddenly a thought struck her. "Listen, Tirzah," she said, grabbing her little sister's shoulders, "I don't want you to tell anyone about what happened with those Egyptian children, all right? Mother wouldn't like us talking to Egyptians, and she would also be very worried about what happened to me. So don't tell yet. I'll talk to Father about it first."

Tirzah nodded her head vigorously up and down. "Yes, Jarah. But—" She stopped.

"But what?" Jarah prodded.

"Why did you do it? I mean, they're Egyptians. They're mean to us. And that girl, well, it sounded like she was apologizing for being mean to you before. And you could've been killed."

Jarah took a deep breath before answering. "Tirzah, I couldn't let that boy be killed when I could do something about it. And maybe now that I have an Egyptian friend we'll be able to help each other. You never know."

Tirzah shrugged. "It just seemed strange. I don't think they'd do it for us."

Jarah sighed. "No. You're right. I don't think they would. But, do you remember what Father said the other night? About loving people who hate us? That's really hard to do, but we should still try."

"Do you... love that girl?"

"I don't know. I do know that I feel sorry for her. Didn't you hear? She doesn't have any friends. And it doesn't sound like she has a mother, either."

"Yes..." Tirzah whispered, hanging her head.

"Come on, we should get home."

The girls hurried home and came bounding into their house, panting and breathless.

"What're you girls doing here?" Mother asked in utter amazement.

"Ada sent us home—because she thought we would—get in trouble," Jarah wheezed.

"What?" Jarah's mother fumed. "What did you girls do?"

Frogs?

"Nothing," Jarah exclaimed defensively. "It's just that the Egyptians might think that we did."

"What did you do? Out with it, girl! What's the matter?" Mother shouted angrily.

"Jarah, she must not know about the frogs," Tirzah reminded her sister.

"Frogs? Jarah, were you playing a trick on the Egyptians?" Her mother's eyes narrowed as she looked into Jarah's face.

"No. Honestly, Mother. We didn't do anything. It was just that frogs suddenly came hopping out of the Nile, and everyone in Rameses is panicking. And the frogs are huge!"

"What are you talking about? I think the heat must be getting to your head."

"No, Mother. It's true! Really. Ask Tirzah," Jarah responded matter-of-factly.

"Where's Shayna and why were you sent home?" Their mother was obviously not convinced by what they were telling her.

"I don't know where Shayna is, but she should be here soon. Ada sent us away because the Egyptians might think that we cast a spell or something to make all the frogs appear," Jarah replied.

Mother opened her mouth to ask another question, but before she could, Shayna came rushing into the house, staggering and out of breath.

"Ugh, frogs. I hate frogs!" Shayna cried out in disgust, collapsing into a chair.

"Shayna, are you all right?"

Shayna described exactly what Jarah had just told their mother. Their father, who was lying on his bed, commanded, "Mariel, don't badger the children. If you aren't convinced by what they have to say, go and look for yourself."

"All right. I shall," Mother stated in annoyance as she limped towards the door. "And I want you girls to watch Yanni and Raphael."

When their mother came back her face showed a look of utter astonishment.

"So, it's true?" Father questioned.

"Yes…" their mother's voice trailed off. "It is."

The girls had just finished changing their dresses when Eitan and Lemuel came running into the house, winded.

"We can't work any more," Eitan gasped out, plopping down on a stool. "The mud is so full of frogs we can't even mix the straw, mud, and water together to make the right consistency. And they're so big they keep knocking over things and people. I even saw them knock over a stack of bricks."

Lemuel grabbed a wet cloth and began to wipe the dirt and gunk off of his arms. "I'm hoping this means work is cancelled for another couple of days," he said, jokingly. "I'm so glad that the frogs aren't here!"

"Yahweh is good," Father murmured from his bed.

"Why don't they kill the frogs?" Raphael asked, innocently.

"You can't even think about killing a frog," Mother ordered. "Frogs are sacred."

Raphael stared at her and blinked. "You mean, the Egyptians and you worship... *frogs?*"

"No," Mother said in exasperation. "One of the gods is Heget. She has the head of a frog. Frogs are associated with fertility and resurrection because they come from the Nile. So frogs are sacred because they represent the goodness of Heget. We don't worship frogs. We just hold them as sacred."

Raphael stared at his mother for a moment and then burst into laughter. "You—you worship frogs?" He was laughing so hard that Tirzah and Yanni started laughing with him. It was all Jarah and Lemuel could do to hold their composure and not laugh, too.

"Stop it, all of you. This is a serious matter!" Mother shouted, angered by this offense against her beliefs.

"Children, that's enough," Father said with a smile, slowly moving to a sitting position. "We can talk more about it later. But for now we might make use of the time we have here at home. The fence that holds our oxen and donkeys really needs to be mended." As Father said this he tried to get out of bed, but the effort was obviously too great for him.

"We can do it, Father," Lemuel said, kindly. "Eitan and I know how."

Frogs?

"Oh, but you boys have been working hard for my sake for days," Father began.

"It's fine, Father. We can do it. Really we can. We promise to not over-extend ourselves," Lemuel said, grinning at Jarah.

"Thank you, boys," their father replied gratefully, lapsing back onto his worn pillow with a gracious smile.

"Jarah and Tirzah, take Raphael and go weed our plot of ground," Mother charged them.

"Yes ma'am," Jarah replied wearily. She wished that she could rest but she knew that she needed to help the family, especially since their father was so weak and sick. But as she bent over to pull weeds in the garden she couldn't help but wish that she was their mother's favored child so that she could get the more pleasant jobs. Tirzah's voice interrupted her thoughts.

"I wonder how long this plague will last," Tirzah murmured.

Plague? Jarah thought. *I never thought of it being a plague, but I guess you could call it that.* Aloud she replied, "I have no idea."

"Do you think we'll be free soon?" Raphael piped up. "Papa mentioned something about us going to a land flowing with milk and honey." He licked his lips as if he could taste the sweet food.

"I hope so," Jarah replied with a small giggle at Raphael's behavior. "We'll just have to wait and see. Now hurry up so we can get some more straw after we weed this."

א

Eitan grunted a little as he heaved another log up to Lemuel who was straddling the fence. Together they balanced the log and then shoved it into the grooves that would keep the log in place.

"There's no more wood," Lemuel pointed out, panting a little from exertion. "We'll have to use some of the rope we have left to finish fixing the fence."

"Right," Eitan assented. The boys headed towards the wagon where they kept all of the tools and supplies for fixing things. Lemuel clambered up into the wagon bed and started digging through the mess in search of a rope.

"Found it," he finally exclaimed holding up a nice, long stretch of rope. But Eitan seemed oblivious to what his brother was saying. He was leaning up against the wagon staring out into the pastureland, evidently in deep thought. Lemuel jumped out of the wagon onto the grass.

"Eitan?" Lemuel nudged his brother gently.

"Hmm?" Eitan asked, a little startled.

"I found the rope."

"Oh. Right. Let's go then," Eitan said distractedly, leading the way back towards the fence with strong, quick strides. Lemuel ran up to him and looked into his brother's troubled face.

"What are you thinking about?" Lemuel prodded. "Is something wrong? You haven't seemed yourself all day."

"Oh. No. Not really," Eitan replied, but his mind was obviously elsewhere.

Lemuel let out a long, drawn-out sigh. Dragging information out of his introverted big brother was never easy.

"You've just been acting very serious lately. And you've been going out with father a lot more than usual. I just thought something might be wrong," Lemuel said, casually.

Eitan looked sideways at Lemuel. "You're not going to stop prying until you know, are you?" he asked, with a slightly teasing grin.

"Oh, I'm sure I can guess what you're thinking about since you tell me almost everything sooner or later. I just want to make sure nothing else has come up." Lemuel threw his brother a jesting look.

Eitan chuckled slightly. He knew he could trust Lemuel. Eitan told his little brother practically everything. But no, soon Lemuel wouldn't be his "little brother" any more. Lemuel was already almost as tall as he was. And he was very mature. Chuckling again he turned to Lemuel and said, "Well, what's your guess?"

Lemuel looked at him, a grin on his face. "Ada, right?"

Eitan nodded and Lemuel was pleased to see a smile cross his brother's face as Eitan looked down at the ground and kicked a stone out of his way. "Right."

"Have you talked to her father yet? I thought that was your next step."

"No," Eitan began, a little hesitantly. "I know that Ada's the girl that Yahweh wants me to marry. But honestly, I don't know if I'm ready to be a leader and a provider."

There was a slight pause.

"I think you are," Lemuel said, quietly. "If something ever happened to Father, I think I'd trust you just as much as I trust him."

Eitan turned a beaming face to Lemuel. "Thanks, Lem. That means a lot coming from you."

Lemuel was a little taken aback, not only by what Eitan had just said, but by his bright countenance. Though Eitan was always happy, Lemuel had never seen Eitan beam. "Why?" he asked.

Eitan stopped walking. They were back at the fence now. "Because you know all my faults," Eitan finished with a slight laugh. Lemuel laughed, too.

Eitan grew serious again as he said, "But anyways, that's why I've been going on walks with Father so much. We're talking about whether I'm really ready to be married or not. But soon, very soon, I hope to talk to Jaden about Ada."

"Well, I'll be praying for you," Lemuel said, tying a tight knot in the rope.

"Thanks," Eitan murmured, focusing on his work. "And Lem," he suddenly said, "don't tell anyone else. Especially Tirzah."

Lemuel laughed. "Of course not. Tirzah won't hear a word of it from me. If she even guesses at what you were thinking Jaden will hear about it in three minutes."

Eitan nodded, smiling. "Nothing gets by her, especially nothing that's related to romance." He chuckled. "But now we have to hurry up. It's getting dark and we need to get back."

"THANK YOU."

For many days there was utter destruction in the Egyptian town. During that time Father's strength improved and he was soon well enough to help around the house.

"Father, Father!" Lemuel came running in a few mornings later. "I've just come from the Hebrew marketplace and all the elders said that the frogs are dead. Moses said that he would ask Yahweh to kill the frogs if Pharaoh let us go sacrifice to our God in the wilderness. Pharaoh said he would. So Moses prayed and Yahweh killed all the frogs. We're all going to make sacrifices to Yahweh in the wilderness!" Shouts of joy came from the family.

At last, real, true freedom, Jarah thought happily. *I wonder how long it will last.*

"Hurry, children. We must pack and get ready to leave with the rest of the Israelites," Father instructed.

"I'll go find sheep and goats for the sacrifices, Father," Lemuel offered. He took care of their animals.

"I'll help him," Eitan said, quietly.

"Yes, please do," replied Father. "I'll get the oxen and hook them up to the cart. Raphael, you can help me with that."

"Yes sir," Raphael replied readily, his eyes sparkling.

"Shayna," Mother called, "see to the bread and make sure it's baked. We must have plenty of provisions if we're going into the wilderness. Jarah, take Yanni with you and go to the river and get enough water for our family for at least a week. Tirzah, I'll need your help packing."

"Wait, you actually want to come, Mother?" Tirzah asked in amazement.

"I don't care about worshipping Yahweh, but it will be nice to get out of this infernal heat and go to the mountains," Mother said, with some exasperation. "Now hurry up. Get your sandals on."

"Yes Mother," Tirzah replied.

"Come with me, Yanni," Jarah called. "I can't hold your hand and this jar, so you'll have to follow along and be good or else you'll be in big trouble when we get home."

"Yes, Jah-Jah," the little boy replied meekly, wiping his sticky hands on his tunic before rushing off after his sister.

All through the streets everyone was getting ready to go. People were packing up and there was laughter and celebrating. Jarah hurried through the crowds of people and tried to keep track of Yanni, who was constantly disappearing in the crowd. Thankfully the river was not very crowded and Jarah gladly put her pot down on the ground and shook out her aching arms.

"Phew," she murmured. "Clay pots are heavy."

Jarah was just dipping the jar into the river when she heard a *splash*. Her eyes jerked towards the sound.

"Yanni!" she cried. He had jumped into the river off of the bank and was now thrashing around in water that covered his head. Jarah threw the pot down and ran into the river. She struggled to wade quickly through the deep water but finally reached out and grabbed Yanni's hand. She pulled him from the water. Yanni surfaced, gasping

"Thank You."

for air and clinging to Jarah with all of his might. Jarah picked Yanni up and held him in her arms as he burst into tears.

"Jah-Jah, I wet and cold," Yanni wailed. "I fall in."

"Yes, yes, I know Yanni. Shhh. It's ok," Jarah said trying to soothe him, but she was shaking with fear.

"Jarah, is he all right?" an alarmed voice exclaimed. Jarah looked up to see Ezra sliding down the bank towards where she was standing waist deep in the water. Amissa stood above them, holding two pitchers.

"I think he's fine," Jarah replied, tremulously.

Ezra splashed through the water towards her. "Here, let me take him," he offered, peeling Yanni out of her arms. They waded back towards the beach where Amissa was now waiting for them. Ezra clambered up onto the sand, then offered Jarah his hand and lifted her from the water.

"Thanks," Jarah murmured, gratefully.

"Jah-Jah, I cold," Yanni sobbed, holding his arms out towards his sister.

"I'm sorry, Yanni. It's all right," Jarah said, taking Yanni back from Ezra. The little boy buried his face in her shoulder, crying.

"What were you doing here?" Ezra asked, concern and worry evident in his dark eyes.

"We were getting water," Jarah answered, nodding towards the jar she had dropped on the ground. "I thought Yanni was right behind me, and then suddenly he was in the river." Tears were welling up in Jarah's eyes. She struggled to blink them back.

"Here, let's help you back. I'll take the jar for you," Ezra said, picking the jar off of the ground and lowering it into the water.

"No, really, it's all right. I can get it," Jarah insisted.

"You need to help Yanni. Besides, we live right next to each other. It's not like I'm going out of my way," Ezra stated, lifting the pot.

"But Amissa can't carry two jars," Jarah persisted.

"No, but I can." Ezra walked over to his little sister and took the full jar from her. Amissa hurried to the water's edge and filled the other.

"See? Now we can all go back together and it's no trouble at all. Let Ezra be helpful, Jarah," Amissa said persuasively.

they're just as stunned as we are. I just don't know." Eitan's eyes drifted back to the window.

Jarah turned her head and saw her family working outside in the garden. They looked so happy, so peaceful. She wished that she was strong enough to join them, but she feared it would be several more days before she was up and about. At least she had Eitan as a companion, though he seemed to be doing a lot better after only one day. Her thoughts quickly turned to the poor Egyptians who were experiencing yet another plague. She wondered what it was like, stuck inside a city with swarming bugs. She shuddered, not even wanting to imagine it.

A shadow darkened the doorway. Jarah smiled. "Amissa."

"Shalom." Amissa came in and sat on the bed beside her. "I'm so sorry that you're hurt. I heard what happened."

"Don't worry. I'll be back to normal soon. I just know it," Jarah said, trying to appear better than she felt.

"That's good," Amissa said quietly. But she wasn't really looking at Jarah now. She was looking down, straightening the blanket on the bed.

"Is something wrong?" Jarah asked with concern. Amissa gave a sad, drawn out sigh.

"I guess—I guess I'm just worried about Ada," Amissa replied reluctantly. "Shayna brought a message to us yesterday after she brought cloth to the queen. Ada said she's fine, but the Egyptians are very mad at the Israelites. I'm just worried about her."

"Are the Egyptians really that angry with us?" Eitan asked, abruptly entering the conversation.

"I think so. But Ada said she's all right, so…" Amissa sighed again. "I think I'm just letting my fears get the best of me." Amissa shrugged her shoulders as if she were also trying to shrug off her fears.

Eitan nodded his head slightly and turned away from the girls. But Jarah heard him mumble under his breath, "If the queen's not careful it might be too late for Ada."

Amissa didn't hear him, but Jarah did. She smiled a little and thought, *I wonder, does Eitan really love Ada? He's obviously very worried about her. I hope she'll be safe.*

Jarah looked from Amissa's smiling face to Ezra's tantalizing grin. "Very well," she finally assented. "It would be hard for me to get back carrying a jar and Yanni, especially since I'm soaked. Thank you. And I'm sorry you got wet, Ezra," Jarah finished, apologetically.

Ezra shrugged, still grinning. "It's fine. I don't really mind. It's rather hot today."

Jarah gave him a shaky grin back as the foursome started up the road. Yanni quickly calmed down, and soon asked if he could walk. Jarah put him down and Yanni walked next to her, holding her hand.

They soon entered the Israelite town and were in a large crowd of people. They tried to thread their way through the maze of carts, animals, and baggage. Suddenly there were screams and shouts of terror and the Israelites began to scatter in all directions.

"What's wrong with everyone?" Amissa wondered aloud. Jarah looked towards Ezra questioningly. In Ezra's eyes was a look of panic mixed with anger. Twenty or more Egyptian soldiers abruptly came charging through the crowd with their swords drawn.

"Girls, get back!" Ezra shouted. His face was pale but his eyes kindled with indignation as he gently, yet quickly, pushed the girls towards the wall of a house and stood in front of them protectively. Yanni was clinging to Jarah's leg in fright and Amissa was grasping her older brother tightly by the arm. Ezra dropped the pitchers in the sand and his hand flashed to a dagger concealed under his tunic. Jarah's eyes grew wide. He could be killed for carrying a dagger. The Israelites were never supposed to have any type of weapons. Where did he get it? Ezra prepared to leap upon an Egyptian soldier who was pushing an Israelite man roughly to his knees. Soldiers were everywhere.

"Ezra no! Put it back," Amissa whispered frantically. "It won't do any good. Put it back!" Ezra reluctantly hid the blade but still maintained his protective stance before the girls.

One of the soldiers shouted out, "SILENCE!"

Instantly, silence reigned. Everyone stood in the street as if frozen. Even the animals looked as if they were life-like statues. The Egyptian shouted out again.

"Thank You."

"What are you doing? There's work to be done. The dead frogs in our part of the land must be put into heaps and then burned."

Murmurs of despair and disbelief rose from the crowd. One broad Israelite man stepped forward and exclaimed angrily, "We were told that Pharaoh himself said that we could go to the wilderness and sacrifice to our God. That's where we're going."

"What?" the soldier laughed. "Like we would just let you go. You would surely escape. No. No one is to leave. You're slaves, and will do as we command, or else." The soldier brandished his sword.

"But the pharaoh said we could go," another man chimed in.

"Then the pharaoh must have changed his mind. Now get back to work. This land needs to be cleaned up and made to look like it once was. You can't possibly leave now. And if any of you try to leave or sneak out, we'll have to enforce the strictest punishment." The other Egyptians nodded their heads. "We will be watching you. All of you," the soldier said mysteriously, pointing his sword at the people circled around him. Then the soldiers all spread out and took up different stations from which to watch the Israelites.

For a few moments everyone just stood where they were in shock and disbelief. But no one dared to raise any more arguments. So they quietly melted away.

Ezra sighed and picked up the pitchers again. "Let's go home," he said, dolefully.

"But Ezra—" Amissa began, obviously heart-broken with tears gathering in her eyes.

"Amissa," Ezra interrupted, "we've got to get home. I understand. I'm terribly disappointed, too. But I must get you girls home before we get in trouble."

Ezra looked so grown-up in that moment. His joyful, yet helpful and optimistic spirit was gone. He seemed so drained of passion and energy that Jarah and Amissa obeyed without another word. Yanni, too, seemed completely shaken and clung to Jarah's skirt, though he didn't really know what they had just been denied.

Moisture clouded Jarah's vision as she looked down at the dusty street. She tried to fight back the tears of anger and disappointment. How could the pharaoh have done this? How could Yahweh have done this? She didn't know. And right then, she didn't care, either. She was angry. Really, truly angry. She had walked this street so many times she could probably do it with her eyes shut. She had longed to go into the wilderness and see what it was like beyond this city. And now she couldn't. In fact, she doubted that she would ever go anywhere besides this city. And she also doubted that they would ever be free.

Maybe Yahweh really doesn't listen like Mother says, Jarah thought bitterly. *I thought that He might, but now* — Jarah's thoughts were interrupted as Amissa entered her family's home and Ezra continued on ahead with Jarah to drop off the pitcher of water.

As the three of them entered Jarah's house she could see from the expressions of despair on her family members' faces that they had also heard the disappointing news.

"Where would you like this, ma'am?" Ezra asked politely.

"On the table, Ezra," Mother responded, dryly.

Ezra laid down his burden and with a compassionate yet comfortless smile around the room, he turned and walked out the door. Jarah suddenly remembered something and ran after him.

"Ezra!" Jarah called.

Ezra turned around with a curious expression on his face. "Yes?" he questioned.

"Thank you for helping me, and keeping Yanni and me safe," Jarah mumbled, shyly.

"You're welcome," Ezra nodded, a small grin of appreciation spreading across his face. He quickly turned on his heel and walked away, leaving Jarah alone in the street. Turning towards home, Jarah brushed away the tears and steeled herself for another day of work and more disappointments.

א

For the rest of the day all of the Israelites were employed in cleaning up the dead frogs in the cities of Egypt, piling them into heaps to be burned at sundown.

The days dragged on. Every night Jarah slumped down on her bed, falling asleep before her head hit the pillow. Every day she watched

"Thank You."

with a bleeding heart as her brothers and father came home so weak they could scarcely talk. She wanted to be angry at the Egyptians. But she seemed almost too tired to be angry. She could only dream of the day that she and her family would live on their own in freedom. But it was only a dream. And what Jarah was now living in could only be described as a nightmare.

בּ

One day Jarah was working on cleaning the front courtyard of the temple of the Sun god, Ra. She had been working all day, alone. Usually Tirzah or Shayna was with her, but Shayna was helping her mother weave some cloth that they were late in delivering to the queen and Tirzah was collecting more straw. They were behind in producing the required amount of bricks, again.

Tirzah's probably already done her work, Jarah thought wearily as she cleaned the marble courtyard floor for the fourth time. Every time Jarah thought she was done she found new muddy footprints on the wet floor. She was nearly convinced that a temple guard, who was monitoring her work and the work of the other Israelites, was playing tricks on her, for she knew that she had cleaned the courtyard thoroughly.

As the evening wore on and the expansive courtyard was being cleaned for the fifth time, Jarah was so tired that her arms felt like bread dough. She hadn't had a break all day, not even for water, and her shoulders were burning from the heat of the sun and the constant back-and-forth motion her arms were making. It was getting late and she was starting to feel light-headed from hunger and weariness.

"There, I'm done," she gasped out as she stood on the now immaculate floor. She looked timidly at the overseer and he nodded his head slightly in approval.

"That's good enough," he grunted. "Don't forget to water the plants."

Oh, I forgot about that, Jarah thought hopelessly. All the other Israelites who had been working at the temple had been dismissed for the day and the street was almost deserted. *I bet my family is wor-*

ried about me, she told herself as she dragged the dirty soapy bucket of water to the nearby drainage ditch and emptied it. *I'd better hurry.*

As Jarah tried to quicken her pace by running back and forth to the well for water, she began to feel dizzy and her vision became blurry, making it hard for her to see. *Come on, just one more plant. You can do this,* Jarah encouraged herself. But as she lifted the plant from the shelf on which it rested the heavy pot slipped through her fingers. Vainly Jarah tried to catch it, but the pot had already reached the floor and shattered into a million little pieces.

Jarah stood as if stunned. She had just broken a pot that held in it a plant sacred to the Egyptians. But that was not all she had to worry about. The shadow of the Egyptian guard leaned over her, chilling her to the bone. Jarah spun around and began to beg, "Please sir, I really didn't mean to. I just—"

"You were being careless," the angry man bellowed. "And you'll pay for your mistake." He pulled out a long leather whip from behind his back and with a whine the whip hit her shoulders with tremendous force.

Jarah was knocked off her feet from the intensity of the blow. At the next strike she bit her lip hard to keep from screaming. Doubling over under the blows, Jarah fell to her stomach and feebly held out her hand in an attempt to stop the overseer. Another and another blow fell upon her shoulders. The pain was terrible, but it was just beginning. When the fifth or sixth blow fell, it ripped open the fabric on her shoulder and tore open her flesh. Jarah could no longer hold in her terrified screams. Her body shook from the fierce blows; her voice shook even more with pain and terror. She soon felt that she would faint, but she saw no one who could help her.

But maybe if I do faint, she thought between screams, *he might stop.*

Suddenly she heard an angry voice cry out, "Stop it! You're going to kill her!"

Jarah turned her head slightly and through tear-filled eyes saw Eitan running towards her, his face aflame with a rage and passion that Jarah had never seen before.

Where are Father and Lemuel? Jarah thought. *Eitan's only going to get himself hurt trying to help me.* Aloud, she shrieked, "Eitan, don't.

"Thank You."

You'll only get in trouble!" Her cry was interrupted by another blow from the whip and Jarah finished weakly, "Go get help."

Eitan, however, only ignored her cries and flung himself onto the Egyptian and tried to wrestle the whip away from him. Jarah reached out, grabbed the Egyptian's leg and tried to pull him down. But the Egyptian kicked her and sent her sliding across the wet floor into the wall. Jarah blacked out for a moment. Her vision slowly swam back into focus. Eitan was still struggling with the Egyptian, but even though he was strong he was no match for the guard's strength. The man was hardly shaken as he threw Eitan off of him and onto the stone floor. Eitan fell hard and lay still. For a moment Jarah felt sick to her stomach. She wanted to do something to help Eitan, but she was too weak to do anything but pray he was all right.

Then Eitan moaned. Slowly and painfully he rose to a sitting position and pushed himself up to his feet, trying to regain his composure. The overseer had an evil grin from ear to ear. He picked up the whip and came back towards Jarah.

Eitan shouted out, "No!" and stumbled towards the overseer.

Without warning, the whip changed its course and instead of hitting Jarah it curled around Eitan's bare chest like a snake, hissing and jerking. It wrapped around Eitan's body once, and as the end came around again the overseer caught it in his hand and then pulled the two ends, tightening the coils that surrounded Eitan. The man drew the whip closer and closer in quick, short jerks. Eitan doubled over in pain, struggling to remove the whip from his chest. The whip continued to close tighter and tighter and soon it was impossible for Eitan to breathe. He grabbed the whip and pulled it as hard as he could, trying to wrench it from the Egyptian's hand. Jarah watched helplessly as Eitan's face turned blue and he gradually lost strength. He collapsed to the ground. Leaning over Eitan's fallen body, the Egyptian continued to pull on the whip.

Without warning, Eitan made one last attempt to free himself. He moved quickly and kicked the man in the chest, sending him flying. The Egyptian roared in anger and pain as he hit the wall. He was up in an instant, but in that instant Eitan had freed himself and was now sitting up, gasping for air. With a menacing yell the overseer charged

Eitan and jumped on him. There were a few moments of struggle as Eitan somehow managed to block the man's fierce punches. But it was obvious that Eitan was at a disadvantage. In a split second the Egyptian had knocked Eitan flat on his back and was on top of him, hands around his neck, choking him.

Jarah had no idea what to do. She couldn't run, but Eitan's life seemed to depend upon her doing something. Then, she thought of the one last possibility.

Please Yahweh, if you hear me and ever have heard me, she prayed silently, *let this man listen to me and stop.*

Jarah drew up her last ounce of strength and rose to her knees. The movement sent a wave of pain through her body and she almost passed out. But she was now close enough to lay her hand on the overseer's arm. He turned to her with a cruel sneer and Jarah spoke, though her voice was no more than a whisper, "Please don't do this."

The overseer's face held a mocking grin, but his expression quickly changed when he looked upon the girl and then turned back to the young man. Jarah's face was full of pain and sorrow, but yet, he saw something else in her eyes—something that he had never, ever seen before. He saw love in her eyes. Love for her brother, and love for... him.

At that moment, as much as Jarah had tried to look back on the Egyptian's mocking grin with anger, she could not help but feel a little sorry for him. *All he knows are statues. He doesn't know how to love and he has no one to love him. At least I have my family, even if we don't always get along. If he knew love he probably wouldn't be doing this to us. He would love us instead like, like Yahweh loves us...*

The overseer felt almost overwhelmed with guilt. He looked from this poor, bleeding girl, to the suffocating, self-sacrificing boy whose lungs were heaving for air. Eitan's eyes were glazed over as he stared into the man's eyes, pleading, begging for his life. The calloused overseer could take this guilt no longer. He let go of Eitan's neck and slowly stood up, just looking at Jarah. Eitan rolled free, taking in deep, life-giving breaths.

In a few moments Eitan rose to his knees and looked at the overseer, wondering what would happen next. His sides were still billowing

"Thank You."

from lack of air and he looked very weak, but he was still determined to save his sister. But the overseer wasn't brandishing his whip like Eitan had expected. Instead there were tears in his eyes as he yelled, "Go home!" and ran away.

Eitan was shocked by what had just happened. A low sob from Jarah brought him back from his daze. His chest was burning from where the whip had encircled him. He slowly rose to his feet. Every move he made felt like it was draining the life out of him. He was dizzy and light-headed as he made his way to Jarah and knelt at her side. Jarah's face was full of pain and there were tears of pain and love mingling down her cheeks as she whispered, "Thank you, Eitan." She wrapped her arms around her brother's neck and laid her head on his shoulder, sobbing. Eitan put his arms around her, being careful to avoid her wounds, and helped her up. He didn't say anything, but as Jarah glanced up into his pale face she saw a comforting smile on his lips. He gently helped Jarah to her feet and supported her aching frame as they walked back to their house. Eitan felt the last bit of his strength waning as he struggled to hold up his little sister.

When they arrived at their house, Eitan just barely managed to kick the door open and stumble inside the dark room. There were gasps of horror and astonishment from the family members who had been very worried about them. Now the family's fears were confirmed.

"Eitan, what happened?" exclaimed Father.

Eitan couldn't reply. He only shoved Jarah into Lemuel's waiting arms and sank down onto a stool, breathing heavily. Lemuel gently helped Jarah to her bed. In a moment Shayna was by Jarah's side with some warm water and a washcloth. She slowly peeled away Jarah's bloody rags from the wounds the whip had inflicted and laid the warm cloth around Jarah's throbbing shoulders. Jarah couldn't keep back a scream from her lips as the warm cloth was laid on her skin. It stung her shoulders terribly. Jarah squeezed her eyelids shut to keep the tears from coming.

I must be brave, she thought.

Eitan watched Jarah's pain, feeling the awful sense of responsibility. His mother touched his shoulder.

"Are you all right?" she questioned softly. She, too, had a warm cloth in her hand. She nodded towards the burn that the whip had made around his bare chest.

"I'm fine." Eitan tried to make light of the situation.

"Let me put this on it," Mother commanded.

"Really, I'm—"

"Eitan," his father commanded, solemnly, "it will be better for you later on. Let Mother and Shayna examine you."

Eitan didn't want the pain the cloth, herbs, and oil would add, but he knew that it would probably be best in the long run. However, as his mother gently rubbed the wound it seemed to only be burning him and not helping him in the least. He found himself blinking back tears.

Once Eitan and Jarah's wounds were washed and everyone else was in bed, Father came over to Eitan and demanded to know the whole story. Eitan told it all, with a little hesitation, and also explained that he had been held late at his work, as well. If he had not been given another load of bricks to carry he would not have heard the pot crash and Jarah's screams. As he finished his story his father was silent. Eitan asked, "Was I right in doing that, Father?"

After a slight pause Father replied, "Eitan, you know it isn't right to assault those who are in authority over you. But if as you say the beating was for a small fault, I can't see that you were in the wrong in this case, especially from how bad Jarah looks. But, if she had really done something worthy of punishment, you would have to determine whether or not she was being punished justly or being abused before you stepped in. Do you understand?"

Eitan nodded. "Yes, Father. I understand."

Father nodded and then added, "I'm very proud of you, my son. If for some reason I were to leave this earth before all of my children are married and the girls have another protector, I would be at peace knowing that I have you as such a faithful son to protect and guide them."

"Thank you, Father," Eitan replied gratefully.

"And you know, son," Father continued. "I think today more than proved that you're ready and willing to be a protector and provider.

"Thank You."

Maybe that conversation with Jaden will happen sooner than you think." He gave Eitan a teasing look.

Eitan knew he was blushing as he asked in a quiet, calm tone, "Do you really think so?"

Father nodded and grinned. "You're ready, my son. You have my blessing."

Eitan couldn't stop smiling. "Thank you, Father," he said, trying hard to hide the excitement he felt.

His father grasped his arm and said, "Get some sleep. I know you need it."

Jarah was in too much pain to sleep. She kept replaying the whole scene in her mind. She couldn't help but think about how Yahweh had arranged for Eitan to be there when she needed protection, and how He had turned her heart and the Egyptian's heart towards Him as she had cried out for help. She quietly told herself, "I guess Yahweh does answer prayers, though it may not be in our own timing." She silently prayed, *Thank you Yahweh, for protecting Eitan and me. Please keep us safe as we heal and please let Eitan not be hurt too bad for trying to help me. And also, please help me to learn more about you, and to be able to trust in you. I think I want to trust you. But… I don't know how. Please, please help me. Amen.* Then, with a sweet peace in her heart, Jarah also dozed off to sleep.

A Cry From Egypt

WHOSE GOD IS REAL?

Acenith started up in bed in the middle of the night.
What is that? It sounds like some sort of humming.
She silently climbed out of bed and felt her way to the window. She lifted the latch of the shutter and peeked out. The moon was shining brightly, washing the city of Rameses white. But the humming sound was louder now. What was it?

Abruptly, Acenith gasped. Something was covering the moon. It wasn't a cloud. It was a sort of haze. And suddenly the haze was in the streets. And then it was flying into her face. She shrieked and found that tiny bugs were flying into her mouth. She spat in disgust and immediately closed the window. But the tiny bugs were flying in through the cracks in the shutters. They were gnats. Terrible, annoying, biting gnats. Bes was screaming and she heard her father's drunken shouts.

"Acenith? Get that light! Get something for me. What is this?"

Acenith found her way to the table, knocking over a chair in the process. A candle was still glowing faintly. She grabbed another candle and lit it, illuminating the room. But all she could see was a haze of bugs and her father and brother trying to fight them off. They were biting her, hurting her. She ran to Bes and held him close.

"Another one of these accursed plagues. Ra curse you, you evil, malicious Israelites!" her father roared. He jumped up, threw on his priest's outfit, and cursing and swearing made it to the door.

"Where are you going?" Acenith cried out.

"To the temple to pray for the gods to give us some peace around here," her father stormed, slamming the door behind him.

Bes was crying. "Cenith, I want it to go away. Pwease, pwease make it stop," he wailed.

Acenith held him close, crying with him. "I can't Bes, I can't. No one can. Only the pharaoh can say when these stop. I don't think they will stop until he lets the Israelites go."

א

"It's amazing."

"What's amazing?" Jarah asked.

Eitan slowly and carefully rose from his stool and came over to her. He gently moved the bed so that Jarah could see out of the window.

"Look at Rameses."

Jarah sharply drew in her breath. A moving, hazy, misty mass rested over the city and over all the land, as far as the eye could see.

"What is it?" she wondered.

"Gnats. Hundreds and thousands of gnats. Another plague." Eitan sighed, easing himself back down onto a chair. "I wish the pharaoh wouldn't bring this destruction upon his land."

"But why? Why won't he let us go?" Jarah queried.

Eitan shrugged, then grimaced at the movement. Reaching to adjust the bandage around his chest he said, "Pharaoh's heart has become hardened. It's almost like… like Yahweh doesn't want him to let us go. I don't understand it. Neither do the elders. Father went to see one of the elders this morning when he saw the plague, and

A Cry From Egypt

ב

A few days later work was resumed again, even though the gnats were still around. But they didn't bother the Israelites at all. And soon, Yahweh sent the gnats away.

Jarah exhaled in relief. She was finally up and about, though she had to rest often and her back still hurt. Jarah was making some stew for dinner out by the fire pit when suddenly everything got very dark, as if a huge, ominous cloud had blocked out the sun.

"What?" she asked in surprise. Looking up, she practically screamed. A huge, black, moving shape was spreading out over the sky. And suddenly it shot down towards the city of Rameses. The mass of whatever it was seemed to grow in numbers and not only entered the city but seemed to settle over all of Egypt, except for Goshen.

"What is it? What's going on?" Jarah cried out.

"What? What are you babbling about, girl?" Mother shouted from inside the house. The loom was clacking. She and Shayna were busily weaving cloth for the queen.

"There's something, or a lot of somethings, all over Egypt! They came out of the sky."

"What?" Mother and Shayna dashed towards the door, followed by Yanni and Raphael.

"What's that?" Raphael exclaimed in horror. But no one knew.

In a moment, Tirzah came running towards Jarah from where she had been working on the Nile River digging clay.

"Tirzah, what happened?" Jarah asked, worriedly.

"There's flies everywhere!" Tirzah said in disgust. "They just descended in that big cloud." Tirzah shivered. She had never liked insects.

Soon Eitan, Lemuel, and Father came back from work. It was truly the biggest swarm of flies that they had ever seen in their lives.

"Yahweh is definitely at work once again," their father said. "I've never seen anything like this."

"But why aren't the flies here, Father?" asked Tirzah, innocently.

"Yahweh must be keeping them from us. He is in charge of all things and incredibly powerful. It appears that He believes we have had enough suffering and that the Egyptians need to be taught what it's like. Tomorrow morning Eitan and I will go talk to the elders in the town and see what they have heard from Moses."

ג

Ada ran around the queen's apartment, slamming the doors closed and pulling tapestries over the window. Flies were everywhere. They were flying into her face, practically blinding her. The queen was screaming in terror in the next room. The shrill cries of the maids were echoing down the halls. Ada frantically swatted at some of the flies as she struggled to cover the windows.

"Ada," A Hebrew maid named Lexine ran into the room. "The queen wants you to summon the magicians, quickly. She's terrified."

"Of course. I'll go right away."

Ada pushed open the door and ran out into the hallway—right into a swarm of flies. She tried to shoo away the bugs with her hand, but her efforts were futile. She tried to run, but she could barely see where she was going. Abruptly, she ran into someone, nearly falling over.

"Oh, I'm sorry," Ada gasped, steadying herself against a wall.

"Ada, what are you doing here?"

"Paki?" It was her friend Paki, who delivered messages to her family.

"You should be in the queen's apartments." Paki gently grabbed her arm and helped her to stand up.

"I'm supposed to get the magicians for the queen to see if they can perform some type of magic and get rid of the insects." Ada coughed as she swallowed a fly.

"Let me go. You should be with the queen and out of this terrible mess," Paki offered.

"Thank you. That would be wonderful." Ada smiled up into his face gratefully.

"I'll bring the magicians to the queen in just a few minutes." Paki gave her a half-smile and ran off through the courtyard. Ada saw that he was nervous and worried. She couldn't help but feel sorry for the Egyptians. They didn't understand the power of Yahweh and what

He might do to them if they continued to resist His commands. Ada sighed in despair.

How will they survive? Ada wondered as she hurried back up the stairs to the queen. *What's Yahweh going to do next?*

ד

After breakfast the next morning Eitan and Father left to go talk to the elders. They came back bearing good news.

"Yahweh has put a division between us and the Egyptians. He said so through Moses, who told that to Pharaoh. Pharaoh laughed and didn't believe that a swarm of flies was coming. But now, he's shocked and stunned. He called Moses before him this morning and sent Moses out to make supplication for him and his household. Pharaoh said that if the insects went away he would let our people worship in the wilderness," Father said.

"Do you really think he'll let us go, Father?" Shayna asked.

Father shook his head. "No, Shayna. I highly doubt it. But perhaps Yahweh is softening the pharaoh's heart at last. We must just wait, and pray."

ה

Moses and Aaron walked down the rich, red carpet.

"You wished to see us, Pharaoh?" Aaron asked as Moses' spokesman.

"Yes. I see that the flies have left." Pharaoh, proud, young, and strong, looked out through the great windows into the land of Egypt—his kingdom. The pharaoh chuckled, low and menacing.

"Tell your people that work resumes, *tomorrow*."

"Tomorrow? But my lord, you promised that we could go to the wilderness and worship Yahweh. We told you we could not worship in front of your people for fear of being stoned!" Aaron exclaimed. He was trying to be respectful, but wrath shone in his dark eyes and his face was turning red. Moses' face was immoveable, the Pharaoh noted, with a twinge of annoyance. This Moses seemed to be calm in everything.

"Well, I have changed my mind," the pharaoh shouted. He stared the two men down with deep, penetrating eyes. "Three days is too much time for your people to be away. More crops need to be planted. No. You may not go. And nothing you say can change my mind. Now, go."

Aaron was about to protest but four soldiers surrounded the two men and practically forced them out of the door.

"Yes, Moses and Aaron," Pharaoh murmured darkly. "A couple of magic tricks won't move the power of the almighty Pharaoh. It'll take more than a weakling god to do that."

With a smug and defiant face, Pharaoh snapped his fingers for his attendants. This was going to be a long, busy day. And he was ready for anything that came his way. Or so he thought.

ו

"What?"

Jarah was jolted from her sleep, her heart pounding. Who had called out?

"How could this happen?" a voice shrieked.

Jarah turned to see her mother plop down on a stool, her face in her hands. Early morning light shone through the windows. Father and Lemuel stood in the doorway, sad looks on their faces.

"Father, what's happened?" Eitan asked, slowly rising from his bed.

Father looked down at the ground, his eyes sad. "This morning, all the Egyptian cattle were found dead."

Jarah's jaw dropped open. Tirzah, who had been awakened by their mother's cries, gasped.

"What? How?" Shayna cried.

Father shook his head. "No one knows. Seems like it's some strange disease."

"Lemuel, what about our cows? Are they—" Eitan's face was white.

"No. They're fine. When I heard what had happened I ran to check on them. There doesn't appear to be anything wrong with them."

"Once again, Yahweh has brought destruction on the Egyptians," Father said, quietly. "It's terrible to see so many people suffer because of the pharaoh's hard heart."

"But Father, doesn't this mean we don't have to work today?" Jarah asked, hopefully.

"I don't know. We can't perform some of the tasks we usually do if we don't have cattle, but they might find other things for us to do."

Mother suddenly looked up, her eyes flashing. "Is that all you're worried about? Work? Don't you see what is happening? The Egyptian gods are under attack. Our sacred cattle have been killed. Who's doing this? How can the gods let this happen?" Mother was so angry that she was crying.

"Mariel, calm down. I—"

"Calm down?" Mother shrieked. Tirzah clutched Jarah's arm, trembling. "No, Asher! This is terrible. This is horrible! I'm going to pray." Mother stormed from the hut and disappeared behind the house. There was a long, terrible silence.

"Well," Lemuel finally said, softly, "Mother's right. The Egyptian gods *are* being attacked. But we, unlike her, know who's attacking them. Yahweh is."

Jarah thought about what Lemuel had just said and realized that so far every plague had been a direct attack against the Egyptian gods. First, the sacred Nile, then the goddess Heqet, then the insects that they held sacred, and now the cattle.

"Amazing," she murmured.

"Asher?" Amasai stood at the door. "We still have to work today. Your family better get moving." He was clearly irritated. "The pharaoh's so stubborn. He said he's going to import some cattle as soon as possible. And he'll probably be using some of our cattle, too. Now hurry up. I'll be back soon with specific instructions."

Amasai left and Father sighed again and shook his head.

"Quickly, children. Let's see if there's any bread left from yesterday," he said, grabbing a pitcher of water and putting it in the table. "I'm afraid that we'll be slaves until Egypt is utterly destroyed," he finished, almost as if he was talking to himself.

"You mean we'll never be free?" Raphael's lip began to quiver and Jarah could see a tear in his eye.

"I don't know, Raphael," Father replied, sitting down despondently on a stool and wiping the hair from his brow. "Yahweh is obviously at work. But Pharaoh's heart is hard and stubborn. I'm not sure when Yahweh will change Pharaoh's heart, or what He's going to do next. But we know that He is listening to us and really does care about us."

"He doesn't listen, or care," a defiant voice called out. Mother was standing in the doorway, her eyes still snapping, her face red with anger. "He doesn't listen at all. That's what I've been telling you for the past few years. We must pray to the Egyptian gods for freedom and deliverance."

"But Mother, why would the Egyptian gods let us go?" questioned Eitan.

"They obviously have the power and they know that the Egyptians are in the wrong. That's why all this is happening," Mother stated proudly.

"Mariel, we've discussed this before—" Father began, but she interrupted him.

"The Egyptians are obviously more powerful than we are, so it has to be something about their gods."

"But Mariel," Father said, calmly, "why would the gods who have given the Egyptians great power give us great power, too? For if all of the Israelites left, Egypt would certainly lose almost all of its power. You see? They really can't do anything. They aren't real gods. You see how useless they are to the Egyptians even now. Yahweh is the real God."

Mother stood, staring blankly at her husband. She didn't have anything else to say. Reluctantly she turned away, leaving the conversation unfinished.

"Father, do you think anything will soften Pharaoh's heart?" Jarah queried, setting some bread on the table.

"Yahweh only knows," Father replied with a gesture of her hand upwards towards heaven. "But there's always hope. I haven't given up yet. It's just amazing how severe these plagues are. I know that they are sent from Yahweh, and I know that He is looking out for us. Now hurry up. We need to eat before Amasai comes back."

If Father thinks there's hope then I won't give up either, Jarah told herself decidedly. *Not yet, anyways.*

A HARDENED HEART

Ada smoothed her dress and quietly entered the queen's apartments. The queen was sitting in front of her mirror and one of her maids was rapidly applying eye make-up to her face.

"You called for me, my Queen?" Ada said, submissively.

"Yes. Quickly, get my royal wig and crown. I've been summoned to the court," the queen instructed.

"At this early hour?" Ada asked, more to herself than to the queen.

"Yes." The queen paused for a moment before saying, with a cold edge in her voice, "Moses and Aaron are back."

Ada hurried to the chest where the queen's finest jewels, crown, and head-piece were kept. Now she knew why the queen seemed so anxious. She was worried about another plague.

In a few minutes the queen was rapidly moving through the hallways, Ada at her side, and guards surrounding her. They came to the extravagant throne room and entered through a back door. Ada scanned the crowd as she took her place behind the queen's throne, which was to the left and on a lower tier than the pharaoh's. The pharaoh's face was dark and grim. He was already angry before Moses even entered the room. All of the chief magicians were there, writing on scrolls, mixing potions, and putting incense on the small fire pits that surrounded the room, giving off a sickly sweet scent. Some musicians sat in a corner, playing sad tunes on their reed flutes. More guards than usual had been stationed around the room, guarding all the doors. Ada felt uneasy. She knew that something big was going to happen. This was the first time that Pharaoh had called his queen to be with him when Moses and Aaron came. She had been there the first night, but other than that she hadn't seen Moses and Aaron again.

Suddenly the heavy wooden doors were thrown open. Ada jumped. Moses and Aaron strode confidently into the room and down the rich carpet, staffs in hand, surrounded by guards. Ada noticed that Moses and Aaron seemed to be holding something in one hand, but it was concealed from her view.

Oh no, she thought. *Yahweh, please, can any mercy be shown? Can you please soften Pharaoh's heart?*

Moses and Aaron came up to the dais and Aaron said, "Pharaoh, Yahweh has commanded you to let His people go that they may serve Him in the wilderness. You have time and again ignored the voice of the Lord Yahweh. Now tell us, what will your answer be? Will you again persist in hardness of heart? Will Yahweh again have to show you His awesome power?"

The pharaoh's lips were curled up in a sneer. "I already told you that I don't know your God. And I refuse to let your people go. My magicians have shown that they can imitate almost every plague that your weakling God has sent our way. I am prepared to hold my ground. I will not let your people go."

There was a long, dreadful pause as Pharaoh stared down, long and hard, into Moses' eyes. Moses let out a long, sad sigh. Then he said, "Pharaoh, you have brought this upon yourself and your innocent people." At this Pharaoh's eyes grew a little wider and his face a shade paler. "Behold, the power of Yahweh," Moses finished.

Immediately Moses and Aaron opened their hands and threw something that looked like dark dust into the air. It fell to the floor, softly blanketing the marble in a fine, dark dust. Moses and Aaron

A Hardened Heart

turned as one and left the room. A magician scrambled out from behind his table and ran to where the dust had settled. He touched it with his finger and examined it.

"It's soot, Lord Pharaoh," the magician said.

"Soot?" Pharaoh said, scoffing.

"Yes, sir." The magician rose to his feet, a wicked grin spreading across his face. Suddenly his face turned white. He cried out a little and clutched his hand. The next moment several shouts of pain sounded from the soldiers who had been closest to the soot. The pharaoh jumped to his feet, his face ashen.

"What's going on?" he demanded.

A chorus of voices answered, but Ada couldn't make out what they were saying. She felt the queen clutching her arm.

"Ada, take me back at once," she gasped out.

"My queen, is something wrong? Are you—" Ada froze. Her eyes opened wide with horror. Huge boils, painful and blistering, where breaking out all over the queen's arms. Ada looked into the queen's eyes. They were full of pain and terror.

"Guards, the queen needs to go to her apartments, now," Ada commanded. The queen and herself were quickly surrounded by guards and brought back to the queen's apartments. The queen collapsed on her bed, crying in pain and agony. Ada hurried to get ointment and bandages. All around her the Egyptians maids were breaking out with boils. They were screaming and running around frantically, scratching at the boils and trying to find relief.

"Please Yahweh," Ada whispered as she pulled bandages from a closet, "protect me and let me be a witness to the Egyptians here. I know you put me here for a purpose. Please, let me fulfill that purpose, and give me strength and courage to endure anything you send my way." With that brief, fervent prayer, Ada ran off to minister to those in pain.

א

"Good-morning," Amasai called from the doorway.
"Shalom. You look well," Father called back.

"I am well," Amasai replied, jovially. "Work is postponed."

A chorus of cheers arose from the family members. Tirzah and Raphael danced around the room and Yanni screamed in delight. But Mother rose from her stool in the corner and demanded, "Why? Why has work been postponed?"

"Another plague. Yahweh once again has worked a miracle through Moses and Aaron. Early this morning Moses and Aaron threw soot in the pharaoh's presence. The soot caused boils to break out on all the Egyptians. They are in so much pain and agony that they can barely walk. Until they are well enough to tell us what to do, I believe we'll have a much-needed break. I'll let you know when work is resumed in full swing. It would be wonderful if your family could bring in some more straw to the market place over the course of the day, but other than that you have no other obligations. Good-day," Amasai said as he headed for the door.

"We will. Good-day, Amasai," Father shouted after him.

Freedom. Oh thank you, Yahweh! Jarah's heart soared until her mother shouted at the younger children.

"Quiet, all of you! I've had enough of this, this celebrating over the doom of the gods. All of you, get to work and get out of my sight! I have cloth to weave." Mother plopped down at her stool and began weaving cloth. The loud clacking of the loom quickly forced everyone out of doors.

"Father, what did Mother mean? Did something else happen to another Egyptian god?" Tirzah asked as she skipped up to where her father was preparing the wagon to get more straw.

"Well, Tirzah," Father began, swinging Tirzah up into the back of the cart, "I'm not well versed in the Egyptian gods. But I know your mother prays quite frequently to the goddess Bast. I believe she is supposed to be the goddess of joy, health, and healing, and is supposed to give protection against contagious diseases."

"Are the boils contagious?" Tirzah asked, innocently.

Father nodded. "Usually boils are very contagious. They can also be painful. We must pray for the Egyptians to be healed. Can you do that?"

"Yes sir. I guess they don't have very powerful gods, do they?" Tirzah queried, furrowing her brows.

Father grinned as he picked up the ox-goad. "Well, the Egyptians gods aren't real, so they technically have no power at all," he explained.

"Father, can I come, too?" Jarah questioned, running up beside the wagon.

"Of course." Father grabbed her hands and lifted her into the wagon.

"You're strong," Jarah said with a giggle.

"Not really," Father replied, tweaking her nose with his finger. "You're just little."

"I'm twelve. I'm not little. I'm almost a woman," Jarah protested.

"Yes you are, but you'll always be my little girl to me," her father insisted. He smiled on her fondly, tucking a stray strand of hair into her head-covering. He turned away and struck the oxen on the back, heading them out to the marsh. Jarah laughed as the wagon bounced up and down over ruts and holes.

"Yahweh, thank you for letting us be free, just for one day. And thank you for showing me your power," Jarah whispered. "I—I think I *want* to trust you with everything in my life. But I still have some unbelief and fear, too. Can you help me with that, please? Amen."

ב

Pharaoh chuckled, a low, deep, menacing chuckle, as he saw Moses and Aaron again approaching him. The first rays of sunlight were stealing into the throne room and made the red carpet glow eerily.

"I see that the boils have finally gone, Moses," he said, laughing aloud. "Your God doesn't seem to be able to let these plagues last for more than a week. I believe it is clear that our gods have been able to give us back our health."

Moses shook his head and replied, softly, "Pharaoh, how long will your heart be hardened?"

"As long as you and your wretched brother persist in playing these games with me and demanding that I let your people go!" Pharaoh spat, enraged.

Aaron stepped forward, strong, determined. "Pharaoh. Thus says the Lord, the God of the Hebrews, 'Let My people go, that they may serve Me. For this time I will send all My plagues on you and your servants and your people, so that you may know that there is no one like Me in all the earth. For if by now I had put forth My hand and struck you and your people with pestilence, you would then have been cut off from the earth. But, indeed, for this reason I have allowed you to remain, in order to show you My power and in order to proclaim My name through the earth. Still you exalt yourself against My people by not letting them go. Behold, about this time tomorrow, I will send a very heavy hail, such as has not been seen in Egypt from the day it was founded until now. Now therefore send, bring your livestock and whatever you have in the field to safety. Every man and beast that is found in the field and is not brought home, when the hail comes down on them, will die.'"

The pharaoh's face was dark with hatred and anger. He leaped from his throne and practically screamed, "No one tells me what to do! You get out of my sight! If you dare to speak such words to me again, you will feel the consequences!"

Before Moses and Aaron could say anything more soldiers surrounded them and forcefully escorted them from the throne room. Pharaoh sat back on his throne, breathing heavily. Pharaoh's advisor and the prince's tutor, Panhsj, waited a moment before approaching the throne. With tremulous steps, Panhsj knelt in front of the pharaoh. "My lord?"

"What is it?" Pharaoh snapped.

Panhsj took a deep breath and started rubbing his hands together, nervously. "Shouldn't we consider what Moses and Aaron have said? If another plague is on its way, shouldn't we take precautions and keep the few cattle and animals we have and our servants safe?"

The pharaoh turned dark, flashing eyes upon his advisor. "Have you grown soft, Panhsj?" he said in a low, dangerous tone. Abruptly he rose and shouted out to the court, "Listen to me all of you. If you have that much doubt in our gods that you don't think they can protect us from a little hail, then fine. Go lock up your precious belongings. But I say to you that the pharaoh shall not lock up his cattle and his servants. To do so would be to admit to the world that I am afraid of a god of slaves and doubt my own strength and power. I am the morning and the evening star. And I wield strength and power. Everyone to the temple to pray. We will ask the gods to once again protect us." Pharaoh stomped down the stairs of the dais and out of the door towards one of the many temples, surrounded by many courtiers and guards. Panhsj still knelt on the marble floor, his sweaty hands still working against each other.

"Panhsj, will you not go pray to the gods?" another advisor asked him.

"No, no… not yet. I'm going to tell my servants to get my cattle and goods stored away… what little is left of them," Panhsj said, standing slowly.

"Are you out of your mind? Didn't you hear what Pharaoh said?" the other advisor exclaimed, his eyes wide with wonder and fear.

"Yes, I did. But he said that if we wanted we could put our animals and goods away. And that is just what I plan to do. I've seen enough to know that this Yahweh isn't a God to trifle with. If you have a sensible head on your shoulders, you'll do the same."

The other advisor stood rooted to the spot. He rarely saw Panhsj this bold, this immovable. Could he make a stand for what he believed? Did he really believe that his gods didn't have power any more?

"No, I can't," he murmured. Avoiding Panhsj's gaze, he fled down the stairs and towards the temple. Panhsj sighed and then hurried from the court. He had much to do before tomorrow morning.

א

"Ada? Ada?"

Someone was shaking her. Ada groaned a little and tried so hard to open her eyes. She was so tired, so weary.

"Ada, it's Lexine. You need to wake up. The queen needs you."

Ada forced her eyes open. Sunlight was streaming through the windows. She had overslept.

"I'll be right there," she muttered, groggily. Lexine darted away to the queen as Ada pushed herself off of her bed and stumbled towards the chest where her dresses were kept.

"Yahweh, give me strength. Give me energy," she murmured, slipping a white dress over her head. "I praise you that I didn't get sick with the boils, but there were so few Israelites and so many sick Egyptians. I've worn myself out helping them. Please, please be my help now."

Ada splashed water over her face and pulled her hair back with a jeweled comb. She breathed in deeply, feeling a little more refreshed, and definitely more peaceful. She was almost walking with a spring in her step as she entered the queen's apartments.

"My Queen, you look so much better today," Ada exclaimed.

"Yes, I think the boils have left at last," the queen said, but she didn't seem very happy. She looked worried. "Please, Ada, get my most ornate wig and jewelry. The pharaoh has asked me to pray at the temple. It sounds like Moses is threatening to call another plague down on us. We must pray fervently for protection."

Ada quickly obeyed the queen's commands. As she adjusted the wig on the queen's head, she whispered softly, her voice shaking, "If I may be so bold, your majesty, I'm afraid that your gods won't provide you the protection you need. Perhaps, if you let me pray with you to Yahweh, He will not inflict another plague upon Egypt."

The queen took a deep breath, then rose and faced Ada. She was scowling and looked very proud and regal as she threw her shoulders back and looked Ada in the eyes. Her expression was cold as she said, "Ada, you know how I feel about you speaking about Yahweh to me. I ask you to remember your position and remember my command to refrain from talking about Him to me. I have respected your request and not forced you to go to the Egyptian worship services with us. Now you must respect my request. Is that understood?"

Ada bowed her head and curtsied in reverence. "Yes, my lady. I understand. Please forgive me for overstepping my position."

"Very well." The queen made a little gesture with her hand, dismissing Ada. "Make sure my lunch is ready when I return, Ada," she called after her as she marched out the door, surrounded by her many Egyptian maids.

Ada shook her head. Tears stood in her eyes, but she blinked them back. The queen had often responded in a similar way when Ada spoke about Yahweh. She was very close to the queen, and the queen hadn't been an unjust mistress. If only she could help the queen see the truth.

Still despondent, Ada walked towards the kitchen to order the queen's lunch.

"Good morning," a friendly voice said.

"Paki. I was hoping to run into you," Ada said, making an effort to be joyful.

"Oh really?" Paki was giving her a curious look. The way his eyes met hers made Ada feel uncomfortable.

"I have a message for my family. Can you deliver it for me?"

"Of course. What would you like to say?"

"Tell them that Yahweh has given me strength, that I didn't get sick with the boils, and that the queen is feeling much better. Also, let them know that I'm praying for them and that I miss them."

"I think I can do that," Paki said, grinning. He was staring at her in that weird way again. "I can't go today, though. My father needs help with some repairs on the pharaoh's chariot. Is it all right if I deliver it first thing tomorrow morning?"

"Of course. I don't mean to inconvenience you in any way. If you're not able to, I can just wait and—"

"Oh no. It's really all right," Paki assured her. "I'd be happy to do anything for you."

Why is he looking at me like that? Ada couldn't help but wonder. She was feeling very uncomfortable.

"Thank you, Paki. I must be going now. I have a lot to do before the queen returns. Good-bye." Ada hurried away, feeling awkward and confused, and just a tiny bit worried, too.

"Good-bye. I'll see you soon," Paki called after her.

"Right," Ada whispered, hoping that Paki wasn't thinking of her as anything more than a friend. She barely knew him. He just helped her out from time to time, though she appreciated that he had been so kind and serving.

"Maybe you're just imagining it," she told herself, and then quickly dismissed all other thoughts on the matter. It was time for her to throw herself into her other tasks and stop thinking about weird looks from young men.

ז

Jarah set the table for breakfast, hoping Father and Eitan would be back soon. Mother was in a sour mood and it was making everyone nervous. She heard footsteps at the door and turned eagerly, hoping it was Father and Eitan and not Amasai. Work had started up again two days ago and the foreman had been coming early so that they could catch up on work. To her relief, Father and Eitan entered. But then Jarah gasped in surprise. In between them was a young Egyptian man who was badly battered and bruised. He was wearing the linen skirt of a servant, but he seemed too young to be working as an overseer. He was not armed, not even with a whip. And Jarah thought that he looked slightly familiar.

"Asher, who's that? And why is he here?" Jarah's mother exclaimed. Egyptians never came into Hebrew houses.

"It's a young man who was on his way to Goshen when a huge hail storm started. He continued to run until he got to our village. However, when he got here, nobody would help him. We will help him. I'm ashamed that the Israelites should be so unkind and inconsiderate. Shayna, mix up some herbs and get some cool water. We'll put that on his bruises to help with the swelling and pain," their father commanded.

"Hail?" Mother said with a disbelieving laugh as Shayna hurried to do as her father asked. "What are you talking about?"

"It's true," Father declared. "There's a huge hail storm taking place in all the land of Egypt, except for here. The hail stones are the size of our clay cups. It's incredible. Everything is being utterly destroyed. It's almost as if fire were raining down upon the Egyptians along with the hail. I have never seen anything like it in my entire life."

"Here you are," Eitan said cordially, handing a cup of water to the young man, who looked to be about his own age.

"Thank you," the young man murmured as he lifted the clay cup to his lips and drank deeply. He was tall and handsome, and his face

A Hardened Heart

looked softer than the cruel overseers'. Everyone was so quiet that Jarah could hear a fly buzzing about the room. Shayna had finished crushing up the desired herbs and handing them and some water to her father, who made a poultice out of it and began to apply it gently to the man's bruises. Shayna stood by, ready to assist. She was a good nurse. Other than Father and Shayna, no one else moved or said a word. They just stared at the Egyptian.

Where have I seen him before? Jarah wondered. *His face looks so familiar.* She then noticed that Lemuel's brow was furrowed like he, too, was trying to remember something.

When he finished applying the poultice Father asked, "What's your name, young man?"

"My name is Paki, and I am very grateful to you and your family for your kindness," the young man replied. He gave Jarah a friendly smile.

Oh, it's the Egyptian that helped me and Lemuel out of Rameses that night when I was caught by the soldier. He seems so nice and kind, not like most of the other Egyptians.

"What kind of work do you do, Paki?" their father continued, trying to make conversation.

"I'm a servant in the palace of the Pharaoh," Paki replied. "I came to Goshen this morning to deliver a message to Jaden from his daughter, Ada. He lives close by. Do you know Jaden and Ada?"

At the mention of Ada's name from this young man's lips, Eitan's face turned a little bit paler and he paid rapt attention to the Egyptian's words. Jarah took special notice of his reaction.

"Yes. They're our neighbors. Now that you mention it, I believe I've seen you come to their door a few times," Father stated.

"Yes. I frequently deliver messages from Ada to her family. Since she's the queen's personal attendant she can't leave the queen's side. I have good standing as a servant, and my father is Pharaoh's charioteer. Thus I'm free to come and go often, and I enjoy helping Ada."

"I'm grateful you're looking out for the Hebrews' best interest," Father said gratefully as he offered Paki some more water.

Paki rose to go. "Thank you again for your kindness, but I really must be going."

"Are you sure you don't want to stay here until the storm passes?" Father asked, a little worriedly.

"No, but thank you for your offer. I will go to Jaden's house and deliver Ada's message and then see what is to be done from there. Again, thank you for your kindness." And with a slight nod of his head he left, though very slowly and appearing a little disoriented.

There was a long pause before Father said, with forced joyfulness, "Well, he was a nice young man. And because of this hail storm I doubt we'll be working today. It's truly a miracle how the hail is all around us. You should all go to the street and see for yourself."

Everyone hurried outside. Jarah drew in her breath in astonishment.

"Oh my," she heard Lemuel murmur at her side.

A thick curtain of torrential rain and hail surrounded the land of Goshen. Jarah could see it stretching for miles. It was dark gray and menacing. Jarah saw huge stone-like things falling from the sky. If she could see the hail from this distance, it must be huge. Lightning flickered across the sky and Jarah could heard the low, deep rumble of thunder starting in the distance.

"It's definitely a work of Yahweh," Father said, coming up behind Jarah and laying a hand on her shoulder. "A little while ago there wasn't a cloud in the sky. Eitan and I saw the mass of clouds appear so abruptly that we didn't know where they came from. It's phenomenal."

Everyone nodded their heads and agreed with Father. Jarah heard a soft noise and turned to see Mother crying and shuffling into the hut. Father saw it, too, and exhaled sorrowfully.

"Eitan, let's go talk to Amasai and see what is to be done today. Lemuel, until I get back, take the boys and go look after the animals. Shayna, you and the girls help your mother until I return."

"Yes sir," Shayna said, going back inside after her mother.

"Are you well, Eitan? You look really pale," Lemuel said. Jarah looked into Eitan's face. He didn't look right. He looked worried, and maybe a little vexed and angry.

"What's wrong?" Jarah asked him, a little alarmed.

"Nothing, nothing much. I'm just thinking," Eitan replied, quickly. He was trying to be nonchalant, but it wasn't working. Jarah could hear tension in his voice. But before she could ask anything else, Eitan spun on his heel and followed their father, still looking a little dejected.

I wonder what's wrong with him, Jarah thought. *Maybe, does it have something to do with Ada?*

ו

It was evening. The hail storm was still raining down upon the land of Egypt, everywhere except for Goshen. Eitan climbed up one of the rolling hills behind their house and plopped down on the ground. He needed to think. His head was in a whirl, even though his face remained tranquil. He knew that he would never, ever forget today.

This morning, on his walk with Father, they had decided that Eitan was ready to ask for Ada's hand in marriage that very day. That's when they found that Egyptian, Paki, staggering down the street and decided to help him. And that's when Paki talked about Ada. Eitan couldn't help but feel worried. This young man was obviously very attractive and kind, and he seemed to do favors for Ada all of the time. In spite of his injuries, Paki's face lit up when he mentioned Ada's name. Was he wooing her? Did Ada like Paki?

Eitan had been rehearsing what to say to Jaden all day long, and the conversation which had just taken place had gone very well.

"Sir, I would like to ask your permission to marry your daughter, Ada. I've watched her for years and her beautiful spirit, serving ways, and love for Yahweh drew me to her. Yahweh has told me that Ada is the girl I should be pursuing. I promise I will protect her with my very life, and cherish her above everything else. Do I have your permission to marry her, sir?"

Though his heart had been pounding and his face was as white as a sheet, Eitan had been able, by Yahweh's grace, to stay calm and reserved through the whole talk. Jaden had been elated and had given Eitan permission almost immediately, saying that he had been observing Eitan's character for years and was more than willing to give Ada into his care. But, there was a problem. Well, several actually.

First, Ada was at the palace all of the time. Jaden hadn't seen Ada in over six months. Eitan and his family were very lucky to be able to see her almost every week, but Eitan rarely saw her without anyone else there. They both knew that getting private messages back and forth would be very difficult.

And another thing. Since Ada was the queen's personal attendant, Jaden doubted that she'd be allowed to marry. He suspected that the queen didn't want her favorite servants running off, getting married, and starting a family. Then they'd be of no help around the palace.

And then there was Paki. Jaden was not sure of this, but he suspected that Paki wanted a relationship with Ada. It was just something that Jaden could sense, deep down inside. Paki seemed a nice enough young man, but as Jaden had said, "The thought of me giving my daughter in marriage to a pagan is horrible. And as long as it's in my power, she'll *never* be his bride." But the problem was that it was *not* in Jaden's power. Ada was in the palace, which was where Paki spent his days. It made sense that if Ada was allowed to marry at all that she'd end up marrying someone who worked in the palace.

Eitan let out a long breath through his nose and ran his fingers through his hair. For once, he didn't know what to do. He could only hope that Ada wouldn't agree to marry Paki and would somehow be able to marry him, instead. But how was he even supposed to tell her his intentions? How was he supposed to get permission from the queen? Dozens of plans ran through his mind.

Could he possibly get a job at the palace? That planned seemed to be laced with difficulties. Even if he could get a position, who knew where he'd be working and if he'd ever be able to see Ada? Very few Hebrew males worked in the palace because of security reasons. And if they did, they were the lowest class of slaves – nothing important enough to be around the queen's ladies in waiting.

It was at times like these that Eitan desperately wished he was educated enough to write. If he could write a note, he could slip it into Ada's hand the next time they went to deliver cloth. But he couldn't write, and he didn't know anyone who did.

Again he sighed. He'd waited so long to be given permission to marry the beautiful young lady, and now that he had permission it seemed like every way of access to her was cut off. He felt absolutely hopeless, and very upset and alone. What could he do? There had to be some way of getting Ada out of this situation.

Then Eitan suddenly realized something. He'd been sitting here, feeling miserably helpless like he couldn't do anything, and he realized he could do something. He could pray. Of course! Why hadn't he thought of that before? Surely Yahweh would know how to get him and Ada together. After all, Yahweh was the one who had planted a desire for Ada in Eitan's heart in the first place.

Feeling a little more relieved and at peace, Eitan poured out his soul to Yahweh as he had never done before. It was hard for him to reveal his deepest emotions. It always had been. But when Eitan was done praying and stood up to go back to the house, he felt like a different man, and he was glad he'd laid bare his soul before Yahweh at last.

The hail storm lasted about a day, and when it was over all the flax and barley fields were completely destroyed, as it had been about time for them to be harvested. The Egyptians were devastated. They would have to spend a lot of money to get enough food to last until next harvest. Also, they traded a lot of their food to get other luxuries from the neighboring kingdoms. How could they keep up their trading status without that food? However, the pharaoh again hardened his heart, for it was just time to plant the wheat. Surely they would get a good crop of that. But that was hardly a comfort to the poor, ruined Egyptian nation.

How much more will it take until the Egyptians let us go? Jarah pondered as she brought some fruits and vegetables to the queen a few days after the storm. The pharaoh had ordered the Israelites to provide food from their own gardens for the people in the palace. Several families had given some small additions of food to Mother, and they now had enough for the queen for several days while the Egyptians were waiting for more food to be imported.

Eitan had offered to accompany Jarah to the palace. He silently strode by her side, deep in thought. He'd hardly said a word since they left their house. Jarah guessed that Ada was on his mind. Perhaps she would be able to tell when they got to the palace tonight.

As they traversed through the town they saw destruction on every side. The streets were full of holes and its immaculate appearance was gone. Many roofs on the houses had caved in. Structures made of sticks were completely demolished. There was hardly a green thing to be seen and an eerie silence reigned in the streets. They didn't talk much, for they didn't want to break the suffocating silence. The shadows were now beginning to lengthen and they both mechanically began to pick up their pace so as to get back home before it was dark. The silhouettes of ruined buildings fell across their path, giving the whole city an ominous air.

They turned a corner and Jarah saw Acenith's house. She clutched the bread that she had stuffed in the sash of her dress. It had been leftover from dinner. The boys had rushed outside without taking it, so Jarah had cautiously asked her mother if she could have it.

"You might as well," her mother grunted. "It won't last 'til morning."

Jarah had put it in her sash, hoping to give it to Acenith and Bes. She was sure they needed some food.

As they neared Acenith's door, Jarah said, "I'm going to run over here for a minute."

She turned towards the house, but Eitan didn't seem to hear her. He kept walking down the road.

"Umm, Eitan?"

"Huh? What?" Eitan started a little and looked at his sister in bewilderment.

"I'm going over here for a minute," Jarah said again, smiling a little at Eitan's bewilderment.

"Oh. Sure," Eitan muttered, lapsing back into silence.

Jarah ran over to Acenith's house and knocked on the door. In a moment the door opened slightly and Acenith's small face appeared. She looked like she'd been crying and her face was pale, pained, and weary. But her expression brightened quickly upon seeing Jarah.

"Jarah. What're you doing here? It's so good to see you again."

"It's good to see you, too. How's Bes?"

"Good, but hungry. We usually get food from the temple where my father performs his services. But, well, no one has the money to spend on sacrifices. And, well, Father's been drinking. We had some wine saved up and he's been very drunk for the past several days. I don't know what to do." A big tear rolled down Acenith's dark cheek.

"Well, I can't stay. We're bringing food to the palace. But I saved some food from dinner. Here. I want you to have this." Jarah took the large chunk of bread from her sash and gave it to Acenith.

A radiant and beautiful smile burst like sunshine across Acenith's face. "Oh Jarah. Thank you so much. May the gods bless you."

Jarah grinned. "Well, I'm glad to help. But, I don't think your gods will bless me. I believe in the one, true God. His name is Yahweh."

Acenith wrinkled her forehead as if she was confused. "I've heard of Him. He seems so different than our gods. Is He really more powerful than ours?"

"Oh yes," Jarah said emphatically. "I'll have to tell you more about Him later. My brother and I need to get to the palace and then get back home before our curfew time."

"All right. I'll look forward to it." Acenith smiled that beautiful smile again. "Thank you, Jarah. I hope to see you again soon."

Jarah nodded, smiled, and darted back up to join Eitan.

"Who was that?" Eitan asked, a little distractedly.

"Her name's Acenith. I met her a couple of months ago. I've seen her a couple of times since. I wanted to give her some of our food. She has a younger brother who needs it."

Eitan barely acknowledged what she said. Jarah was a little hurt. Usually Eitan took a great interest in her friends. But now he wasn't saying anything. Where had the encouraging side of her big brother gone?

"Eitan, is something wrong?" Jarah asked, a little hesitantly.

"No. Not really. Why do you ask?" Eitan shot her a side-long glance.

"You just—you just don't seem very happy. And usually you're more interested in what I do." It was hard for Jarah to say that, but she felt it had to be said.

Eitan shrugged. "I'm sorry. I guess I'm just not feeling myself today," he explained, vaguely. He didn't say anything more and so Jarah fell silent, too.

Finally, the brother and sister reached the small kitchen courtyard. It, too, was hardly recognizable. None of the finery had escaped desolation. There were only a few pieces of shredded cloth left from the soft embroidered cushions. None of the plants were alive. Their withered bodies lay smashed and bruised on the stone floor. There were bits and pieces of broken pottery everywhere, and the fountain was not playing. The courtyard was very gray and dark, not sunny and cheerful as it usually was.

Eitan stepped up to the door and knocked. The hollow sound resounded through the stillness and seemed to last for an eternity. The door swung open. But instead of Ada's lovely, hopeful face, there was another cold, dark one. Jarah quickly recognized it as the face of Tehara, the cook. The cook took the food and muttered a despairing, "Thank you." She turned away quickly and started to close the door. A quick look of panic crossed Eitan's face, but he composed himself almost immediately. Stepping forward very calmly, Eitan put a firm hand on the door to keep it open. Tehara glared at him.

"Is Ada here?" Eitan asked in a quiet, steady voice. "We usually see her when we come to deliver things."

"She's busy and cannot be seen," Tehara responded coldly, and she slammed the door.

Eitan let out a melancholy sigh. Jarah, too, felt rather rumpled from this encounter.

"I wonder if she's all right," Eitan said under his breath. Then he turned to Jarah and said, "Wait here. I'm going to try and find her."

"Eitan, please don't," Jarah exclaimed in terror.

"Why not? Don't you want to make sure she's all right?"

"But you haven't seen inside the palace," Jarah protested, frantically. "It's huge in there. You'll never be able to find her without being discovered yourself. And if you're found, you'll certainly be punished. Please don't. It's bad enough that Ada's in there. I don't want both of you in there, not knowing what's happening to you. And besides, you can't leave me out here alone."

The last point decided the matter for Eitan and he slowly nodded and whispered, "You're right." He sighed again. "Let's go home."

Silence again enveloped them as the pair made their way back through the gathering gloom and ruined houses.

"Eitan," Jarah finally ventured, "you really like Ada, don't you?"

A slight blush colored Eitan's face. He smiled a soft, thoughtful smile and replied, a little hesitantly, "I like Ada very much. She's a beautiful young lady… inside and out." His smile grew bigger.

"Do you love her?" Jarah queried, almost in a whisper. She hoped that wasn't pushing it too far.

Eitan stopped and looked at her. But yet he seemed to be looking past her, too. There was a faraway look in his eyes. "Yes," he murmured. "With all my heart."

Jarah couldn't hide the grin that stole over her face. "That's wonderful. Are you going to try and marry her?"

Eitan looked away from her and started walking again. "I got Jaden's permission. But Yahweh is going to have to perform a miracle if he wants me to marry Ada. I don't know how I'm supposed to get in to ask her. And there's the very likely possibility that the queen will say no. And, well, I think that there are other young men in the way," Eitan finished. He sounded sad now, almost disheartened.

"You mean Paki?" Jarah asked in surprise.

"Yes," Eitan answered simply.

"Do you think he loves Ada, too?" Jarah asked soberly, hardly wanting to hear what Eitan's response was.

Eitan shrugged. "I don't know. And at this point, I'm powerless to control anything. It's in Yahweh's hands, Jarah." Jarah could hear a heaviness in Eitan's voice as if he was carrying a great burden. Then, he continued.

"If Ada wishes to marry Paki, I won't stand in her way." He seemed almost relieved to say that.

Jarah was rather taken aback. "That's—that's very selfless of you, Eitan. You must really love her."

Eitan smiled at her—his first genuine smile of the night. He quickly grew solemn again as he said, "Please, Jarah, don't tell anyone about this. Father and Lemuel know, of course. But I'd rather keep it a secret until we see what Yahweh works out. I especially don't want Tirzah to know. She'd tell everyone in Goshen," he said, giving her a knowing look.

Jarah laughed aloud. "I promise I won't tell anyone, especially Tirzah," Jarah vowed, flashing her brother a big grin. She was thrilled and honored that Eitan had confided in her.

"Thanks," Eitan said with relief, grinning back.

ADA

It was getting late as Jarah struggled up the hill behind their house with a bucket full of water. A very strong wind had been blowing from the east all day long, making work difficult. Jarah's hair whipped in front of her face. Water sloshed from the bucket. She paused for a moment to look at the beautiful sunset that was painting the sand dunes in the distance yellow, pink, orange, and purple. Clouds of sand rose and fell with the strong wind. Jarah was relieved and delighted to see a green mist spreading out in the distance where before there had only been brown, ugly dirt. The hail and the other plagues had destroyed everything that had been growing. Now, grass was slowly coming back and the leaves were growing on the trees. Jarah shook out her arms and lifted the bucket again. She needed to get inside and get to bed. Work had been very hard the last couple of days.

Suddenly, something filmy seemed to cover the sun. Jarah looked up, alarmed. A huge, silver, glittering cloud was rushing towards her. Jarah screamed and ran for the house. Water splashed all over her as she ran with the bucket and entered the house, frantic. Everyone had already noticed the cloud and were looking through the windows. Jarah noticed that the wind was getting stronger. Tirzah was shouting, "What is it? What is it?" and Yanni was crying.

Then Jarah heard a humming sound. A buzzing sound. It was getting louder.

"Oh no," Jarah heard her father say.

"What? What?" she cried, elbowing her way through her siblings and to the window. The buzzing sound was right above them now, passing over their house and descending into the plain behind Rameses.

"Locusts." Their father uttered the dreadful word. "I've never seen so many, as long as I've lived. It's another plague."

"What do locusts do?" Tirzah asked innocently, biting her lip.

"They're like giant grasshoppers. They eat everything green," Father explained.

"But—but the grass and leaves were just growing again," Shayna protested.

"Am I Yahweh to ask why this is happening to the poor Egyptians?" Father asked, sighing. "The poor people. If only Pharaoh would soften his heart."

"Or the gods would take control and stop crushing their own people," Mother suddenly said, angrily. "This is again something to do with the gods. Every one of your so-called plagues has had something to do with an Egyptian god or sacred animal. This time, it's locusts. Ugh!" Mother cried out in anger and desperation and marched outside of the hut to the fire pit, slamming the door behind her.

"Mother was just telling us the other day why the locusts were sacred," Raphael told Father, his eyes wide with fear.

"Oh Raphael, they aren't sacred. They have no more power than any other animal. Yahweh made all the animals just the way He wanted them to be. He didn't make any kind more special than the other kind. His great creation of the animals is supposed to point us back to worshipping Him, not worshipping the things that He's created."

"But then why did Yahweh make animals that eat all the plants, like locusts?" Raphael asked, pouting a little.

"It didn't start out that way. Adam and Eve brought sin into the world. That sin caused creation to fall and animals started eating each other, or destroying things. It's because of us that bad things are all around us now. Yahweh just uses those bad things to show His power, or teach us important lessons. Does that make sense?" Father pried, tenderly and gently taking his little son onto his lap. Raphael nodded again.

"Just remember, all of you, that Yahweh has a plan in all of this, even though we might not see it yet. Just like He brought Joseph to Egypt to save His people, I'm sure He is using this for the good of His people and to display His glory." Father looked around the room at all his children. Then his eyes rested on Jarah as he finished, "He *always* has a plan."

א

It was early morning, the day after the locusts had been taken away by a strong west wind—at Moses' command. And they had left behind utter devastation. Pharaoh sat on his throne, a scowl resting on his strong, handsome features. The pharaoh was young and determined, angry and restless. When things weren't going his way, everyone in the palace knew it. So much time was being wasted by these plagues. And nothing seemed to be appeasing the gods. Had he not felt the terrible pain of the boils? He was almost healed now, but he would have scars on his arms and legs for the rest of his life. And what about the food? Everything was gone: all the crops for the year, all the food he had just imported. The locusts had eaten everything. They had even gotten into the storehouses.

The door to the throne room opened. Pharaoh sighed in exasperation as he turned to see who had come. He didn't want to talk to any courtiers today, and especially not Moses and Aaron. He wanted to go make sure the overseers were doing their duty. But his face quickly lighted up in a slight smile as he saw one of his best friends, Ammon, his charioteer, walking towards him. Two soldiers followed slightly behind him as he came up the royal carpet and bowed low before the Pharaoh.

"Ammon. What brings you here, my friend?" the pharaoh exclaimed with evident pleasure. He motioned for a low chair to be pulled up besides his ornate throne and bid Ammon to take a seat in it.

"Well, it's a sort of favor I ask of you, my Lord," Ammon said, a little hesitantly.

"Oh?" Pharaoh lifted an eyebrow, curiously.

"Yes. You see, well, you remember my son Paki, do you not?"

"Oh yes. Your son is a strong and good-looking young man, not to mention a faithful servant."

"Well," Ammon continued, slowly. "He has found a young woman he wants to be his wife."

"That's wonderful!" Pharaoh exclaimed, quite excited about seeing the young servant with a family.

"Yes, but the lady he has set his mind on to be his wife is Ada, one of your wife's maids I believe, sire."

"Ada…" The pharaoh's brow furrowed. Then he said, "Yes. Quite beautiful. May I congratulate your son on his excellent choice."

"Well, sir, that is why I've come to see you," Ammon said. "Since she is a servant, we need your permission for the marriage. And we need the permission of your queen."

"I certainly give my blessing. I will also talk to the queen directly before I begin my work for the day." Pharaoh called a servant to him and gave him instructions to bring the queen to him immediately, and that it was to be a private audience. Turning back to Ammon he said, "It's a good thing that Paki wishes to keep everyone together in the palace." The pharaoh seemed quite pleased, which made Ammon very relieved. But he also noticed that Pharaoh seemed quite distracted.

"Thank you, my Lord. You are most generous and kind. I will tell my son all that you have said and eagerly await a message from you once you hear from the queen." Ammon rose, bowed low once again, and left Pharaoh feeling much happier than he had before.

Ada

ב

When Ada presented herself early to the queen, she found only Lexine in the queen's chambers.

"Where's the queen?" Ada asked in surprise.

"She's in an audience with Pharaoh," Lexine told her.

"With the pharaoh? Why did she not want me to come? I usually go with her everywhere," Ada said, more to herself than to Lexine.

"It was supposed to be a private audience, I believe," Lexine said with a shrug, bending over her needle-work. Ada sighed a little and hurried to the queen's sitting room to make sure everything was in readiness for breakfast. She had just returned to the bedchamber when the queen entered, looking very pale.

"My Queen, what's the matter?" Ada asked with some alarm as the queen sat down heavily on her bed.

"I… I need some water, Ada. Quickly," the queen panted out.

Ada dashed into the sitting room and came back in an instant with a glass of water. The queen drank deeply and then seemed to calm down a bit.

"Is there nothing I can do for you?" Ada asked softly.

"Yes. In a minute, I want you to come on a walk with me."

"But, my Queen, what about your meal? You look like you need some nourishment."

"No, no. I'm fine. I don't want to eat," the queen replied, shortly. "Give me my wrap, Ada, and let us be off."

In a minute the queen and her servant were walking down cool, marble hallways towards the palace garden that over-looked the Nile River. The queen was silent and Ada wisely remained silent, too. The queen's face was hard and cold. Ada knew something was dreadfully wrong.

They turned into a wide corridor and saw a royal entourage coming towards them. It was the queen's son Rameses, the heir to the throne. At the young age of fourteen the lad was strong, tall, surprisingly handsome, and very clever. He was accompanied by Panhsj, his tutor, and two servants carrying scrolls and the prince's weapons. Four guards surrounded the prince, keeping him from harm. The queen's eyes lit up as she saw her son. The mother and son advanced towards one another, both showing little emotion, but Ada knew that they were thrilled to be together and truly loved each other. According to royal custom, the two rarely saw each other and weren't allowed to show their affection.

"My queen." Rameses bowed in reverence.

"My son." The queen nodded her head in acknowledgment. "How are you fairing? How is your instruction progressing?"

"I'm well. Panhsj has taught me much and says that I'm ahead of the other princes and princesses in my learning. We're on our way to the stables to drive chariots and practice with my bow and arrows."

"Then go, my son, and may the gods watch over you and protect you," the queen said, a soft smile spreading across her face.

Rameses bowed again and then looked up into his Mother's eyes. Ada read longing, sorrow, and loneliness in his eyes. She felt compassion for him. The life of the heir wasn't easy.

"Good day, your majesty," the prince said quietly. He straightened and strode down the corridor throwing a last, long glance towards his mother.

"Goodbye," the queen whispered. She gave a long, forlorn sigh and Ada saw the queen blink back tears. Then she drew in her breath sharply, threw back her shoulders and said, "Now, on to the matter at hand."

The queen walked towards a fountain that was shaded by a small dome of marble. Ada lamented the fact that all of the plants that had once surrounded this private place were gone. The queen knew that here they would not be disturbed and sitting down gracefully on the lip of the fountain, she exhaled deeply and motioned for Ada to join her.

"Ada," she began at length, "I have had some very unexpected and disturbing news from my husband, Pharaoh. And, it involves you."

"Involves me?" Ada almost shrieked, jumping to her feet in shock. "What have I done, your majesty?"

"No, no, my child. It is not something you have done. But it's still something that concerns you," the queen assured her.

Ada

Ada slowly sat down and took a deep breath before asking, "How so, my lady?"

"You know of Ammon, my husband's charioteer, do you not?" Ada nodded her head. "Ammon has been in the palace since he was a mere child. He and Pharaoh practically grew up together. And so, Ammon has always been close to Pharaoh's heart and wishes. Well, this morning, Ammon approached Pharaoh about you becoming the wife of his son, Paki." Ada gasped but the queen went on. "Pharaoh thinks that it would be an excellent match and you would both be able to still serve at the palace. But… I had hoped you would never marry. I want you always by my side, and if you were to get married and have a family then you would not be able to be as faithful to me." The queen paused for a few moments and Ada tried to calm her thoughts.

Paki? How can I marry him? He's a kind, honest young man, and a true servant. But, he's an Egyptian! He worships the Egyptian gods whole-heartedly. How can I marry him?

"What did you tell Pharaoh, my Queen?" Ada asked, surprised at the peaceful tone that she was able to force into her voice.

"I told him my concerns. But he seems very set on the marriage."

"Then, is there still any hope? Any possibility that I might not have to marry this man? I would much rather marry within my own people or just stay unmarried and serve you, my Queen," she added, hopefully.

The queen shook her head sadly and gazed out over the Nile. "I'm afraid there is no hope. I will try to talk to him again, but my husband's word is law. He is able to *make* you marry."

Tears of shock and sadness formed in Ada's eyes. She quickly blinked them back, but the queen still noticed.

"Ada," she reached out and touched Ada's arm in a very motherly fashion, "I know this comes as a great shock for you. I was shocked, as well. But Paki is a good man. If you must marry I would much rather have you marry inside the palace. But I will talk to my husband again and try to persuade him otherwise. I can promise you that. Since he has been so distracted recently, perhaps we will have enough time to change his mind."

"Thank you, my Queen. You are kind," Ada replied with a forced smile.

ג

The rest of the morning and afternoon dragged on like an eternity for Ada. She felt miserable, but had to act joyful. She tried to think about whether or not she should ask leave to visit her family and tell them the news or just send another message.

In the late afternoon storm clouds rolled in off of the sea, making everything dark and rather cool. The queen complained of a headache and lay down, sending Ada off to get some herbs and water for her. Finally Ada could have some time alone to think and pray.

Why me? Why did Paki choose me? What will I say? What will I do? Oh Yahweh, please, don't make me marry this man. Please save me from being married to a pagan, she prayed as she walked back from the kitchen through the dark passages of the palace. Though Ada hardly wanted to admit it, she had always admired Eitan. But since she was in the palace and he was just a common slave, she knew that no relationship could exist between them. Still, when she compared Eitan to Paki she knew that Paki was not what she desired in a husband.

Abruptly the sound of pottery shattering on the floor startled Ada. She peered into the darkness.

"Hello? Who's there?"

The next instant an arm was thrown around her neck, holding her tightly. Ada struggled but couldn't move. She started to scream but a hand was clamped over her mouth. She felt cold metal against her throat. She craned her neck backwards and saw the dark skin of an Egyptian man.

"Prepare to meet your death, Hebrew dog," he spat out.

Ada panicked. She hardly realized what she was doing. She kicked her attacker as hard as she could. A low grunt of pain escaped the man and he relaxed his grip on her. Quick as a flash she was free. She threw his arm into the wall and heard the knife clatter to the floor. Then she darted down the hallway. But the Egyptian had recovered himself quickly and was right behind her.

"Help!" Ada screamed. "Somebody help me!"

Someone stepped out in front of Ada, blocking her path. She shrieked. But whoever it was grabbed her gently and moved protectively in front of her. He put an arm out to guard her. Ada turned to see the first man charging down the hallway. He stopped abruptly on seeing Ada behind her protector.

"Get out of the way, Paki," the man growled. "This has nothing to do with you. That Hebrew dog needs to die so that the gods can be appeased." Ada gasped as she realized who her savior was.

"I think this has everything to do with me, Heru." Paki's voice was surprisingly nonchalant. "You see, I happen to believe that the Hebrews have nothing to do with this nasty affair, and I know that this young lady is especially innocent. Furthermore, I'm not going to stand by and let her be murdered in cold blood. So, I suggest you go on your way before I call the guards."

"Why you little—" Something akin to a roar escaped Heru's throat. He flew at Paki with the rage of a wild animal. Paki held his ground until Heru was practically on top of him. Then a knife seemed to leap into his hand of its own accord and in a moment the two men were engaged in a life or death duel.

"Guards, guards!" Ada cried, pressing herself up against the wall to stay out of the way of the flashing blades.

Suddenly Heru reached out and pushed Paki into the wall with his spare hand. The dagger was coming down towards Paki's chest. Ada couldn't breathe, couldn't move.

The next moment was a blur. Paki threw himself forward and down into a roll, knocking Heru off balance. Heru fell heavily to the ground and the knife flew from his hand and landed at Ada's feet. Ada instinctively reached out and grabbed it while Paki at the same moment leapt upon Heru's back and put his dagger against Heru's neck.

"One move and you die," Paki hissed, panting from exertion. Heru lay perfectly still but he uttered foul curses under his breath. Ada heard footsteps echoing down the hall.

"The soldiers are coming," she breathed in relief.

As Heru heard this he made one last effort to escape. But Paki grabbed Heru's arms and pinned them behind Heru's back with one hand, still keeping the dagger against his opponent's neck.

The guards came rushing down the hallway. When Ada saw them, utter relief swept over her. Her knees felt weak and she sank to the floor. Her head was spinning and she found it hard to see. She barely heard Paki explain rapidly what had just happened. As if in a daze she saw three guards leading Heru away. Abruptly, everything was quiet and Paki was kneeling next to her.

"Are you all right?" he asked in concern. Ada didn't trust herself to speak. She simply nodded. She was trembling all over and tears were threatening to spill out of her eyes.

"Are you sure?" Paki pressed.

Ada nodded again, choking back a sob. "Y-yes," she whispered. "Thank you," she sobbed out.

Paki gave her a half-grin. "You look quite stunned. Here, let me help you back to your chambers."

Paki grabbed both of her hands and slowly helped her to her feet. Ada's heart was still pounding and she realized that she was truly crying and not just sobbing any more. She clung to Paki's arm, barely able to stand. She felt dizzy and thought she might fall.

"Shh, it's all right. You're safe now," Paki said, comfortingly. He slowly led her through the hallways, supporting her and helping her along the way. Before Ada fully realized what was happening a guard was opening the door to the queen's apartments. There were exclamations of surprise from the women inside as Paki assisted Ada in and guided her to a chair.

"Ada, what has happened? Are you hurt?" the queen exclaimed.

Ada shook her head and swallowed. She tried to speak but Paki placed a hand on her shoulder and spoke for her.

"She has been attacked by an Egyptian servant. He has been captured and some guards have taken him to prison."

"What?" the queen gasped. "Who was it? He will certainly be killed for laying a hand on my servant."

"His name is Heru, my lady. He has been a guard here for several years. I've known him to be a very superstitious man and I think he believes, as do many of the servants here, that the Hebrews are causing the plagues. I'm glad I heard Ada's cries when I did. Heru attacked her in a quiet corridor and the guards would not have come in time," Paki explained.

"Paki, how can I ever thank you enough?" the queen said in excited tones.

Paki just shrugged and said, "It was nothing."

Lexine had been attending to Ada, giving her water and examining her scratches and bruises. Ada could feel a little bit of color coming back into her cheeks.

"I believe that Ada is fine, my lady, but a little stunned, as any girl would be," Lexine reported to the Queen.

"Good," the queen said with a sigh of relief. "Paki, did you say that there are others in the palace that feel the same way about the Hebrews?"

"Yes, my lady, I'm afraid there are. Though I doubt that many of them would take drastic steps like Heru did."

"But others might? Do you really think that there's danger for Ada, and possibly Lexine, right here in the palace?" the queen fretted.

"There is that possibility, my Queen," Paki replied, nodding his head.

The queen clutched her heart and fear filled her eyes. "I must send out a decree at once that if anyone lays a hand on one of my slaves that he shall be instantly put to death. Do you think that will dissuade these horrible men?"

"Possibly, my Queen. But there could be other men who were in league with Heru and will do anything to avenge his execution and carry out the deed that he desired to do. Until a trial and inquires take place, we can't be sure that Ada will not be attacked again."

The queen was now anxiously pacing the floor. Ada was starting to regain her composure, but all this talk about people waiting around dark hallways for the sole intent of killing her made a pang of fear drive deeply into her heart.

"What do you think I should do for Ada's safety, Paki?" the queen asked at length. Ada was surprised by the amount of trust she was putting in this young man.

"I have no right to tell your ladyship anything," Paki began softly, "but I would humbly suggest that Ada, and possibly Lexine, be sent back to Goshen for a short amount of time until formal inquiries can be made. None of the people in the palace, besides your ladyship, my lordship, and myself, know where Ada and Lexine live. There I think they will be safe until we find out who was involved with this conspiracy."

The queen stood still, staring off into space, tapping her finger against her leg. Finally she said, "Yes, Paki. I do believe you are right." The queen quickly turned towards Paki and said, "Go get several guards that you know you can trust for a strong escort. And please tell Pharaoh that I request a private audience with him about this matter. Come back here when everything is in readiness and please escort Ada and Lexine back to their homes. Dismiss the soldiers once you get to the border of Goshen so that they don't know of my servants' whereabouts."

"Yes, my Queen." Paki bowed respectfully and turned to go. Ada was finally able to collect her voice and she called out after him.

"Paki?" He turned to face her. "Thank you. I know I wouldn't be alive if you had not come in time."

Paki smiled, a very nice smile, Ada noted. "You're welcome. I was glad to be of service to you." With a parting smile, he left.

"Lexine, go quickly and pack some things for Ada and yourself. I expect you'll be gone at least overnight. Ada, try to rest and enjoy yourself in Goshen. I'm loathe to part with you, but I believe with all that has happened today that Paki is right. Just sit here until the escort is ready. You look quite shocked, poor child."

"Thank you, my Queen. You are too kind," Ada murmured. Her thoughts were swirling. She was really going home. Home—away from this wonderful but horrible place and all the terror and new things it held for her.

"WILL WE EVER BE FREE?"

"Jarah, Shayna," Mother called, "I need to give Yanni and Raphael a bath tonight. Take two clay pots and go to the well down by the Nile River. That one is bound to be less crowded. Please be quick."

"Yes Mother," the girls responded, picking up the clay jars and heading towards the Nile.

The air was cool and crisp, fresh from the rain that had washed away all the dust that afternoon. There was not much happening that evening. *Everyone must be resting for work tomorrow,* Jarah told herself as they walked through the sandy streets. As they turned down a side street they saw two young ladies a little farther ahead of them, talking quietly together and heading towards the Nile River.

"Look Shayna. It's Amissa and Ada." The two girls picked up their pace and soon came up behind their friends.

"Shalom," Ada exclaimed cheerfully, but Jarah noticed that she was a little paler than usual. "I haven't seen you ladies in quite some time."

"We didn't know you were back," Shayna said. "When did you return?"

"I just came back this evening. And I won't be staying long."

"Why not?" Jarah asked.

"The queen needs me," Ada answered, rather sadly.

"How did you get to visit?" Shayna asked.

"Well, some people have, let's just say, ill thoughts of me," Ada replied, hesitantly. A worried look crossed her usually happy face.

"What happened?" Shayna gasped, voicing Jarah's question as well as her own.

Ada paused, then seemed to make up her mind to tell them the story. "I was attacked by an Egyptian servant who was angry with the Hebrews. Thankfully a young Egyptian steward saw him and stopped the man from hurting me. My attacker was arrested, but the queen thought it would be better for me to get away from the palace until the execution and investigation take place."

"I'm glad you're unharmed," Shayna breathed out in relief. "I would be scared to death if something like that happened to me."

"Well, I must admit I was pretty shaken at first," Ada began. "But I've given my fear over to Yahweh and I know that He will protect me. And though I'm not completely at peace, Yahweh has made it very clear that He's not finished with me yet."

"But you're going back?" Jarah asked.

"Yes, I am. I don't have a choice," Ada said, wiping a tear from her eye.

"We all want her to stay here, but if we refuse our whole family will get punished and Ada will be taken back anyway," Amissa put in. "So Father said that we must let her go and that we should pray for her all the time."

"I will pray for you, too," Jarah added.

"Thank you, Jarah. But I see that you're going to get water, too," Ada said, trying to turn the conversation to a more cheerful subject. "Let's continue our conversation as we get the water. We don't want to be out after dark. Our families would start to worry about us." The foursome walked out of the side street and found themselves on the banks of the Nile River.

There were few houses in this area; only fields and gardens for the Israelites. A couple of men and boys were working on their plots of ground, but the area was pretty open and free of people. The sun was just sinking behind the sand dunes, and its last rays illuminated the warm sand in golden colors and made the Nile River glow. The reeds whistled sorrowfully for the now devastated Egyptian people and clung to the girl's skirts as they walked past. Jarah was glad that there was still vegetation in Goshen. The Egyptian land was very dead and dry, with barely a single green thing on it. No sound was heard except for the wind rippling the water and the reed's sorrowful song and the soft tread of their bare feet against the warm sand. The breeze felt wonderfully cool after such a hot day.

Jarah, despite the beautiful evening, began to feel disheartened. Ada was going to be going back to the palace soon, and maybe into grave danger. And then there were the Egyptians. They had gone through all these plagues, and Pharaoh still wouldn't let the Hebrews go. They had been working for so long, and everyone had kept on telling her, 'We will be free soon, just wait and see.' But they were still not free. As a matter of fact, they were far from it. She wondered whether their lives were even safe. Perhaps the threat on Ada's life was just the beginning of threats to the rest of the Hebrews.

"Will we ever be able to see the Promised Land?"

To her horror, Jarah realized that she had spoken her thoughts aloud. Shayna and Ada, who were walking just in front of her, turned around to look at her, questioningly.

"I'm sorry," Jarah murmured with a sigh. "I was just thinking."

"You do a lot of that," Shayna said, annoyed.

"I understand what you mean, Jarah," replied Ada, kindly. "I have often wondered the same thing, and it amazes me that Pharaoh is so stubborn. I just don't understand it… But here's the well." The girls took turns lowering their pots into the crystal-clear water. Ada stood a little apart from the others. The last rays of sun shone on her pale face as Ada looked up towards the darkening sky and at the one, lone star she could see shining.

Ada's so pretty and wise, Jarah thought. *I wish that she was my sister, too. She's about the same age as Shayna, yet she seems older, calmer, and wiser. I guess being a servant to the queen makes her more mature. And she also worships Yahweh and not the Egyptian's gods. I wonder why she's not influenced by their beliefs.*

As Jarah pulled her pitcher from the well Ada turned to her and said, "To continue our conversation, I believe that Yahweh will not rest until He frees us. I believe that He is compassionate towards us and has heard our groaning at last. If we continue to trust Him, He will sustain us and answer our prayers. As for Pharaoh, I think Yahweh has hardened his heart on purpose. I believe that he wants to utterly destroy Egypt so that He can show His greatness to all mankind."

Amissa nodded. It seemed to make sense to her. Jarah also nodded her head, but she was still not quite sure. "I understand. It's just hard for me to believe it sometimes," said Jarah. "And, I mean no disrespect—"

"Oh no. I do not blame you for your doubt," Ada quietly replied. "I sometimes doubt it myself. But I know Yahweh is behind all of this, and I will continue to trust in Him."

At this moment they heard footsteps behind them and turned to see Eitan, Lemuel and Ezra. As Eitan approached, Jarah could see Ada blush and turn her head away, even in the pale evening light.

"Eitan, what are you doing here?" Shayna demanded.

"We thought we should come walk back with you, since it's getting dark. We don't want anything to happen to you since we heard what happened to Ada," replied Eitan, chancing a glance in Ada's direction.

Ada's cheeks flushed again as she said, "Thank you all for being so considerate. You're welcome to join us." Eitan seemed pleased with her reply, and as they all started walking again he took his place in between Shayna and Ada in the front of the group, a hopeful look on his face.

He probably already heard that Ada was back and was just looking for an excuse to see her, Jarah told herself, suppressing a giggle.

Ezra and Lemuel lagged behind. Jarah looked over her shoulder and saw Ezra pluck a reed. He examined it and said to Lemuel, "I think I'll make a reed pipe out of this one, like Father has. I've used his before and wanted one of my own."

Jarah didn't hear Lemuel's reply because Amissa laughed quietly beside her and whispered to Jarah, "I think Eitan and Ada like each other."

"I know that Eitan likes her—" but Jarah cut herself off, remembering her promise not to tell Eitan's secret. Instead she whispered back, "You can tell just by the way he looks at her."

"Will We Ever Be Free?"

"It would be nice if he did marry her. Then you would be my sister." Amissa hid a chuckle behind her hand. "They'd make a pretty match, don't you think?"

"Yes, but do you think it's possible, since Ada's a servant in the palace, that Eitan can get permission to marry her?" Jarah asked, thinking back to Eitan's doubts.

"I don't know," said Amissa, also becoming thoughtful.

Ezra and Lemuel now came running forward to join the group. Suddenly Ezra exclaimed, "Jarah, don't move!"

Jarah froze instantly and Amissa, who was only a foot or two to her right, stopped as well, almost in mid step. Alarm filled Ezra's voice and Jarah heard Lemuel cry out in terror. Jarah turned her head to the side. Just to her left in some of the reeds that bordered the Nile was an asp, curled up a little less than three feet from her, ready to strike. Jarah drew in her breath and tried to remain as still as possible. She looked to see if Eitan saw her danger, but he and the two young ladies had already turned down the street towards their houses and were out of sight.

Lemuel was about ready to panic. He knew that the bite of an asp is both painful and deadly to a grown man, not to mention a young girl. What could he do? If he tried to approach the snake and grab it by the neck, it might get alarmed and bite him or his sister. *What do I do?* Thoughts raced through his mind.

"Ezra, do something," Amissa whispered fearfully as the snake hissed viciously.

"Lemuel, help," Jarah barely gasped out in fear.

"I—I'm thinking Jarah." Lemuel whispered trying to comfort her, but he couldn't keep his own voice from shaking. Jarah could tell from the tone in his voice that he was thinking very hard, but she could also hear the horror and fear that he felt.

Slowly, Ezra reached into his tunic and pulled out the small dagger he kept there for self-protection. *I only have one try so this has to be good*, he thought. Ezra was very determined that neither Jarah nor his sister should be hurt. He brushed his hair back from his eyes and focused hard upon the asp. He pulled back his arm and threw the dagger. It hit the snake, severing most of its head from its body. The snake's body convulsed and twisted, but it was completely powerless. Ezra simply walked up to the snake and finished disconnecting its head. Though the snake's body still struggled, everyone knew that the danger was past. Ezra silently dipped his bloody dagger in the Nile River and then wiped it clean.

As he was doing this, Jarah suddenly felt weak with how close she had been to getting killed and she grabbed Amissa's outstretched arm for support.

Lemuel came up behind his sister and offered her his arm as he asked, "Are you all right?"

Jarah smiled up weakly into her brother's worried face. "I'm—I'm fine. Just a little shaky." Then she turned her head, for Ezra had come up on her other side in case she was going to faint, and with a shy smile she whispered, "Thank you."

He grinned back and said, "You're welcome. I'm glad Yahweh helped me protect you."

Jarah hung her head so as not to show her pale and yet blushing face as Amissa broke out into exclamations of praise and adoration for her older brother. Jarah was very careful to watch where she stepped after that. Neither she nor anyone else ever wanted to be in that same situation ever again.

BROKEN HEARTS

"It was amazing that he thought of that so quickly." Lemuel said, finishing up the story about the incident with the snake to their family members, including Shayna and Eitan, who had missed the excitement.

"Jarah, you were almost killed," Tirzah gasped in wide-eyed fear.

"Yes," Jarah said, shuddering at the thought.

"I'm sorry I didn't notice," Eitan apologized.

"It's all right, Eitan," Jarah responded. Jarah noticed that her voice was shaking. *I'm not doing a very good job of hiding my fear,* she thought, awkwardly. Jarah was sure she was going to have nightmares that night.

"I want you all to be much more careful whenever you go to the Nile River from now on," Father instructed his family. "I'm very thankful that no one was hurt. I think we should all go and thank Ezra for his great service to us. And let us also thank our Lord," he added. Mother rolled her eyes and turned her back on the little circle. Shayna stiffly rose from her stool and busied herself with some dishes.

Father, Eitan, and Lemuel all thanked Yahweh for saving Jarah and Lemuel from the snake.

"Now, let's all go over and thank Ezra," Father said at the conclusion of the prayer.

"Father, could I please stay here? I just feel a little sick right now, and I already thanked Ezra for what he did," Jarah told him. In truth, her stomach was not quite settled. But Jarah also knew that it would be awkward to be around Ezra right now after his 'rescue' of her.

"I think that's fine, if you've already thanked him."

"Yes Father, I did," Jarah replied.

"Good," Father answered, approvingly.

"I'll stay with her, Father, and help get the little boys to bed," Lemuel offered.

"Very well. We'll be back in a few minutes," said Father as he and the older family members went next door.

I hope nobody teases me about this, Jarah thought as she climbed into bed a few minutes later. *It's bad enough that I had to be saved by someone for just not watching where I was going, let alone having it be Ezra.*

Jarah admired Ezra, *just because he's so nice and kind like Lemuel,* she tried to assure herself. Inwardly, Jarah was afraid that when other people talked about the incident they would think that Ezra liked her. Jarah didn't think that Ezra liked her, and she didn't want him to. At least, that's what she told herself. She just hoped her family members wouldn't spread the story around.

When Tirzah slipped into bed next to her that night she whispered in Jarah's ear, "I think Ezra likes you. He was blushing as red as a beet when Mother was thanking him over and over again." Tirzah burst into giggles and tried in vain to suppress them.

Jarah felt her cheeks growing hot and a strange feeling welled up inside her chest. "Listen, you," Jarah hissed angrily, "I don't want you talking about this again to anybody. Do you hear? It was just an accident. Ezra would've done the same thing if it was you or any other girl. And if Mother was thanking him over and over, of course he would be blushing. He's a humble young man, and I don't think he likes me. It's not right to have the wrong kind of likings for people—you know that. Now don't you dare talk about it ever again."

"I guess I won't," Tirzah agreed, a little remorsefully. She thought that the whole thing was quite romantic.

"Tirzah, I mean it," Jarah whispered urgently.

"I said I wouldn't," Tirzah grumbled. She flipped on her side away from Jarah.

"Father? May I go on a walk with you, just for a few minutes?" Eitan asked.

"Yes, of course, son. Good-night everyone. Sleep peacefully," Father bid his family as he blew out the candle on the table. He and Eitan then went out into the night.

Everything was dark and still, but Jarah still had a hard time going to sleep. Even after her father came in she was still tossing and turning. She couldn't get Ezra off her mind. *What's wrong with me?* she asked herself. *I can usually go to sleep right away. I'm probably just too uptight about this.* She turned over to her side again, trying to get more comfortable. Slowly, very slowly, Jarah started to drift off. Vaguely, she heard voices outside their house.

That sounds like Eitan... she thought. Then, she fell asleep.

א

"I'll go inside and get her, Eitan," Jaden said. "But mind you, I haven't had a chance to talk about any of this to her. She's only been home for a couple of hours and we had to finish up chores. I haven't had any time alone with her. So this might be quite a shock to her. Please, be understanding."

"Oh, yes sir. I completely understand," Eitan said, almost stumbling over his words. He was practically shaking with excitement and apprehension. He couldn't tell if his face was pale or if he was blushing brilliantly. He felt tongue-tied and his palms were sweaty.

Jaden nodded, and Eitan saw—with great relief—a look of approval in his hopefully new father-in-law's eyes. "I'll be right back," Jaden said, disappearing inside.

Eitan rubbed his palms together and then quickly smoothed his hair. His palms were sweaty again, and he rubbed his palms on his tunic. His mind was spinning with thoughts and it was all he could do to remember the speech he had determined he would give Ada.

Then suddenly, Jaden was outside with Ada at his side. Though Ada was dressed in a plain brown cotton dress for work, Eitan thought she couldn't be more lovely with that serious, yet pleasant look on her face, her hair tied back behind her head, and the moonlight caressing her beautiful features. Eitan forced himself to keep his mouth shut, knowing that Jaden must do the talking first.

"Ada, I want you to know that Eitan approached me and asked for your hand in marriage." Ada's jaw dropped and she slowly turned to face Eitan, shock and bewilderment in her eyes. "I gave him my full consent, and there's something he would like to say to you." Jaden said this with a slight tremble of emotion in his voice. He backed up and Eitan quickly knelt down in front of Ada and awkwardly took her hand.

A moment of panic fell upon Eitan. He couldn't remember what to say. He looked up in Ada's face and saw on her face an expression he hadn't ever wished to see. It was of horror and fear. Tears were in her eyes and she looked too shocked to even speak.

Eitan found his breath and forced out, "Ada, I love you. I've prayed long and hard about this, and I believe that Yahweh laid your name upon my heart. I—"

"Oh, please Eitan, stop," Ada gasped out. Tears were coursing down her face now. Eitan dropped her hand and looked up into her eyes, feeling absolutely dejected and heart-broken.

"What's wrong?" he asked, in a voice barely above a whisper.

Ada was trying hard to choke back her emotions. She finally succeeded somewhat and turned to her father.

"Father, I haven't gotten a chance to talk to you about what happened today. I so wish I could have before this happened. I told you part of it, but not all." Ada looked from her father to Eitan with a hopeless look in her eyes. Eitan slowly rose from the ground.

"Then, speak out, my daughter," Jaden said, quietly and hesitantly. Ada took a deep breath.

"I told you, Father, that I was attacked, saved by Paki, and then sent home because they needed to make sure they had caught all of the guilty men. But… that wasn't the only reason. I was pretty shaken, not only because I was attacked, but because of something that happened earlier today." Ada took another deep breath. Eitan and Jaden waited, anxiously. "Paki's father approached Pharaoh, asking him for my hand in marriage to his son."

Eitan couldn't suppress a low cry of shock, sorrow, and anger. Ada looked at him apologetically and then hurried on, speaking very rapidly.

"Of course, Pharaoh felt he had to talk to the queen. The queen refused him, but Pharaoh doesn't need the queen's permission. We are all in his power, unless Yahweh decides to miraculously intercede. Paki's father is a life-long friend of the pharaoh and I'm sure the pharaoh won't withhold this favor. The queen and I fear that it's just a matter of time."

Ada now turned and looked Eitan right in the eyes. "I don't know what to do. Paki is a heathen. He doesn't believe in Yahweh. A lifetime of marriage to him would be a nightmare. I can't think of anything else I would rather desire than staying here with you. But, I don't know what to do… If I refuse to marry Paki I will most certainly be executed, or forced to marry Paki, anyway. I just don't know—" Tears flowed from her eyes, and Ada's chest heaved with silent sobs.

Eitan forced his eyes away from Ada's hopeless, tearful gaze and looked at Jaden. Jaden's head was in his hands. He looked helpless.

Eitan looked back at Ada. There was a heaviness on his chest, relieved only by one thing. Ada cared for him. Now, if he could only figure out how they could be together.

"Is there any way that you could speak to the queen about me?"

In a few seconds that felt like hours to Eitan, Ada composed herself enough to say, "I can talk to her, but Pharaoh's word is law. The queen has very little power of persuasion, even if she, by some remote chance, does find favor with my request. But I really don't think the queen would want me to marry anyone outside of the palace. She wants me always by her side, and if I got married to you and started a family I could no longer serve her. I don't know what she would say. I'm afraid she would get very angry."

"Can I get a position in the palace? As a guard, or servant, or—"

Ada shook her head and brushed away a tear. "You know the amount of security. A young girl like me isn't a threat to anyone. A strong young man like you is. That's why they don't allow Hebrew males to work in the palace. I really don't see any way…"

Eitan turned away from Ada and ran his hands through his hair. Tears threatened to spill over from his eyes, but he forced them back.

"Eitan, I'm so sorry," Ada exclaimed, sympathy evident even through her emotion. "I will talk to the queen about you, I promise. I don't love this other man, even though he's very kind and saved me from certain death. He's the nicest Egyptian I've ever met, and perhaps his heart is soft towards Yahweh. But I would never, ever choose a life with him of my own free will." Ada paused, a long, painful pause. Then she ventured, quietly, "Would you want me to refuse the queen? I will if you think it best."

Eitan paced back and forth, thoughts roaring in his ears. He stopped and stared at the stars, trying to think clearly. Ada and Jaden were absolutely silent. Time seemed to move forward at a slow crawl.

Eitan slowly inhaled and exhaled. He knew the answer. He didn't want it to be the answer, but he knew it *had* to be the answer. Having Ada refuse the queen and the pharaoh would mean certain death or forced marriage—two things that Eitan couldn't save her from. Eitan knew what he had to do. He slowly turned around and said, his voice almost breaking, "No. Don't refuse. I've heard how cruel this queen can be towards servants who contradict her will, and I don't want you to be put into danger from something I can't save you from. If this other man is as good as you say, it would be better if you married him. Perhaps that's the way Yahweh will protect you even though I can't."

"Oh Eitan, I'm so sorry. I never meant for any of this to happen."

"Good-night, Ada." Eitan's voice was hoarse and choked with despair. He looked into her dark, pain-filled eyes for one moment, and then turned and disappeared in the shadows. As soon as he knew he could no longer be seen by Ada, he ran through the village and out onto the hill where he buried his head in his hands and sat as still as a stone until morning light.

As soon as Eitan disappeared, Ada promptly burst into tears and ran into the house leaving Jaden alone in the dark, staring up into the heavens and blinking back tears.

"Yahweh, why? Why did you allow this to happen?" Jaden whispered. He sighed, mournfully. "Perhaps we'll never be free, but Ada and Eitan… They both love you. Why must they suffer and break their hearts because of the sins of our fathers?"

A Cry From Egypt

BACK IN THE PALACE

The next morning, Ada was brought back to the palace by Paki, the Egyptian steward. Jarah saw her walking away, but she didn't look happy. Jarah turned to see if Eitan had noticed, but Eitan was sitting alone, looking out the back window of their abode, not seeming to see or hear anything.

א

"Please, my Queen." Ada kneeled at her Queen's feet, her face touching the floor, tears flowing from her eyes. "Please don't make me marry Paki. And please, please consider letting me marry this other man."

The queen didn't look at her beautiful slave. She stared straight in front of her with a hard heart and hard ears.

"Ada, this has all been very difficult for me. I don't want to give you up. But it seems I must give you up completely, or let you marry Paki and still keep you in my service. I know nothing about this other Hebrew, and even though you say amazing things about his character, you know the rule. No Hebrew males are allowed to work in the palace. It's for security reasons. I'm afraid I'm just going to have to obey my husband in this matter so that I don't lose you and can also make him happy."

Ada still knelt on the floor, trying vainly to stop crying. She couldn't help be feel crushed, even though she had already known that the queen would refuse her request. Ada felt all hope within her die as she tried to swallow her sobs.

"Please, Ada, I understand your pain. But it's for the best. Please don't ask me about this again. I can't do anything else for you." The queen's voice was as hard as stone and as cold as ice. Ada stood slowly, wiping away her tears and keeping her head bowed in subjection.

"Yes, my Queen," she whispered, tremulously.

"Now, please prepare my lunch. A couple of our fine noblewomen will be joining me for the meal."

"Yes, my Queen," Ada murmured as the queen dismissed her with a wave of her hand.

Ada practically flew down the corridors to the kitchen to get the food. She really hoped she didn't run into Paki right now. He seemed to always be looking out for her and she greatly appreciated that. But now she just wanted to be alone. It was all she could do to suppress the anger that welled in her bosom. But, it wasn't so much anger as it was sorrow and pain. Ada knew she couldn't be angry with the queen, but she couldn't help but wish there was another way out of this.

"Yahweh, please show me the way. Light my path before me and show me what to do," Ada whispered. Feeling a little relieved, she threw herself into the day's tasks before her, striving to overcome her emotions and serve the queen as she had always done.

ב

A couple of days later, Amissa came late in the evening to tell Jarah some exciting news. A betrothal was being worked out between Paki and Ada. Though Amissa's parents and Ezra didn't seem very happy about the match at all, Amissa seemed thrilled to be getting an older brother.

"He's really nice, Jarah. He's not like most Egyptians. I think Ada will be happy with him. He adores her. He's really tall, and sings and writes very well. He actually wrote a song for Ada. Isn't that sweet? I'm glad he's going to be my brother, though I thought for sure that Eitan was going to get married to Ada. Oh well. He didn't ask, I guess. And… Jarah are you listening?"

Jarah wasn't trying to be rude but she really didn't want to hear her friend's comments. It was nice that Ada was going to be happy enough where she was, but what about Eitan? Eitan *had* asked for Ada's hand. Father had told her so. That was why Eitan had been so quiet and gone off so much by himself the past couple of days. Vainly, Jarah tried to comfort him, but Eitan seemed to have a sorrow in him that would take a very, very long time to heal.

About a week later, Jarah was tucking Yanni into bed when Eitan entered the house. No one else was around and Jarah noticed that there seemed to be a new spring in Eitan's step.

"Eitan, I haven't seen you this happy in a long time," Jarah stated.

Eitan shrugged and smiled a little. "I guess I just haven't had much to be happy about."

"Have you talked with Ada?" Jarah asked, thinking perhaps that the situation between the two of them had been resolved.

"No." A painful expression crossed Eitan's face. But it left just as quickly when he responded, "But Yahweh has given me a sense of peace that's hard to describe. It still hurts, but I will get over it," Eitan finished with conviction.

"I'm so glad," Jarah breathed. She looked lovingly into her older brother's face. He looked almost like his gentle, lovable self again.

It was wonderful to see the desolate expression leave Eitan's face, though Jarah could still tell that Eitan thought often about Ada. He didn't go to see her or talk to her, lest she should arouse more emotions in him which he was endeavoring to hide. Even so, Eitan never did seem to fully recover from his sadness. Jarah often saw him sitting by the window late at night, a blank expression on his face.

Will Eitan ever fully recover and go beyond just having peace to being the happy young man he was before? Jarah wondered, hoping vainly with all her heart that her question would soon be answered.

TRAPPED IN THE DARKNESS

Squish, squish. Jarah's toes stuck to the mud that she and Amissa were mixing with their feet. They treaded up and down on the water, straw, and dirt that made the hard, durable bricks the Egyptians demanded. They had been working for hours with no breaks even for water. Sweating profusely, Jarah felt the moisture dripping from her body. She felt that she could faint from heat and weariness. Jarah's throat felt as dry and hot as an oven, and she would have been grateful for even a few drops of refreshing liquid.

Amissa's hand clasped Jarah's arm, interrupting Jarah's wishful day-dreaming. Her friend was coughing violently. Amissa had been very pale when she came to work this morning. Jarah had asked if she was feeling all right, and Amissa replied that she didn't feel the best, but would be fine. However, Amissa had been coughing all day and working slower and slower. Every time Ezra and Lemuel had come to the pit to get more mud to make bricks they had looked very worried. Ezra seemed loathe to leave his sister, even for a few moments.

On the last trip he had taken, Ezra had whispered to Jarah in passing, "If anything happens with Amissa, I'm close by to help." Jarah had nodded in acknowledgement and was now beginning to think that she might need Ezra's assistance in getting her friend home. She looked very, very sickly.

"Amissa, what's wrong? Do you need to stop?" Jarah asked in concern. She put a supporting arm around Amissa's waist.

"I'm—I'm fine," Amissa sputtered. "I can't stop working. The overseer will beat me if I do."

Jarah's hand strayed to her friend's forehead. "Amissa, you're burning up with a fever. We have to get you home, and quickly."

"What's going on here?" A stern voice sounded over Jarah's head. At the edge of the sand pit above the girls an Egyptian overseer stood, his shadow towering over them.

"Sir, my friend is very ill. She must go home at once," Jarah declared.

"I say who goes home, and when," the overseer snorted. "Now get to work, and speed up the process. You both have a lot more work to do before nightfall."

"Yes sir," Jarah replied meekly.

The man continued to watch them closely. Amissa tried her hardest to keep up with Jarah's quick feet, but she soon collapsed from fatigue. Jarah tried to pull her up, but Amissa sank deeper into the mud.

"Come on, Amissa. Get up," Jarah urged.

"Get up, girl. Hurry up with it, or I'll have to use my whip," the overseer threatened. Amissa struggled to rise, but every effort seemed to drain more strength from her body. Her eyes were glazed over with pain and exhaustion.

"Amissa!" Ezra came running towards them as fast as he could through the thick mud.

"Ezra, she's very sick. We need to bring her home."

"Back off, girl, and you too, boy. Your nation causes enough trouble with these plagues without being lazy on the job. As long as the girl can stand, she'll work. Now get back, or I'll teach all three of you a lesson." The overseer drew his arm back to deal a strong blow with his whip.

"Stop it. Leave them alone," Ezra yelled in desperation. His face was glowing with passion as he quickened his speed to reach Jarah and Amissa.

Suddenly a strong, chilling wind sprang up. The land grew dark, as if the sun was covered by an ominous cloud.

"Eh? What's that? A sand storm?" The Egyptian turned to see what was happening. It wasn't a sand storm, or even a rain cloud that obscured the sun's light. It was something much more terrible. Above them a wall of thick blackness, like a curtain, spread out as far as the eye could see. And it was descending down towards the ground.

"What is it? What's going on?" Shouts of confusion and terror filled the air.

"It's another plague. Run for your lives!" an Israelite man yelled above the other noises surrounding Jarah, Amissa, and Ezra

The soldiers and overseers started to panic. All Egyptians feared the darkness. In fact, the main idol they worshiped was the Sun God, Ra, who supposedly gave them their light. Prayers and cries to Ra were heard through the shouts of anguish from the Israelites. Jarah's heart was pounding. How could they avoid this plague? What was the darkness, and how could they get back to Goshen with Amissa being so weak?

"Come on. We need to get out of here, now!" Ezra exclaimed. He began to pull Amissa from the mud. "Help me!" he cried to Jarah. Together they pulled Amissa to her feet and then half-carried, half-dragged her towards Goshen. Eitan and Lemuel soon caught up with them and Eitan picked Amissa up in his arms. They ran as fast as they could, but the darkness was enveloping everything around them.

"There. We're almost there," Lemuel encouraged. In a moment they stepped into Goshen. The wall of blackness stopped right at the outskirts of the Israelites' land. The group stood as if stunned. What had just happened?

Jarah's eyes darted around. The thick curtain of blackness rose on every side of them, encircling the land of Goshen. Miles away Jarah could see the darkness rising up in the distance. The sunlight shone brightly where the Israelite's land lay, but everything else was covered in blackness. Yahweh had made it night everywhere but in Goshen.

The darkness was so thick that she couldn't see five feet into it, and the only sound Jarah could hear were very faint cries and screams. The whole group stood there, panting hard from exertion and staring at the black wall for several long minutes.

"Praise Yahweh," Eitan finally whispered in awe.

A grin began to spread across Lemuel's face. "You know, before it was the Israelites who were trapped—now it's the Egyptians who are trapped."

Everyone suddenly felt relieved and laughed aloud. Even Amissa managed a weak giggle. The only one who didn't join in the laugh was Ezra.

"We shouldn't be rejoicing in the Egyptians' calamity," Ezra said, a little sternly. Suddenly, his handsome face was as white as marble and he stared ahead of him, not seeming to hear or see anything.

"Ezra, what's the matter?" Jarah asked in alarm.

Ezra stood frozen for almost a full minute, then muttered hoarsely, "Ada's in there."

א

In the palace a few days later, Ada walked slowly and silently through the dark corridors. In her hand she held a lamp filled with oil, but the flame could barely penetrate the thick blackness. For a very, very long time Ada had hardly left the queen's side. No one had dared to move, and everyone had been hoping, praying that this perpetual nighttime would just melt away. But it would not.

"Yahweh, please keep me strong. Help me be able to encourage the Egyptians, especially the queen, and the other Israelites here," Ada whispered in a barely audible voice. A vision of the queen's face flitted through Ada's mind. The queen did not like the dark, and being in the pitch blackness was incredibly trying to her. She had torches and lamps all around her room, creating a small warm glow. Unfortunately, the blackness was so heavy and thick that it weighed down on everyone.

Ada stopped at a fork in the corridor. Which way was the kitchen? She was going there to try to get something for the queen's refreshment.

"I think it's this way," she reassured herself, but she still felt rather frightened, small, and alone. The air was so thick that her voice didn't echo through the hallways like it usually did. She couldn't even hear the *thwap, thwap, thwap* of her sandals against the cool marble floor. It also took great effort to breathe the stifling air.

A faint glimmer of light shone in the distance. It looked like several torches bobbing up and down. A group of soldiers, or servants? Ada peered into the darkness, trying to see who was approaching her. She felt a distinct feeling of dread rising within her. Thoughts of being almost murdered went through her mind.

In a moment, she saw a group of six guards surrounding a boy and an older man. Ada quickly stepped aside, bowing low. It was Rameses, the heir, with his tutor, Panhsj.

"Who's that?" one of the guards demanded, raising a light to reveal Ada's face.

"I'm Ada, the queen's personal attendant. I'm going to the kitchen to get food for the queen."

The guard grunted approval and prepared to move on when someone called out, "Wait." Prince Rameses stepped forward. Ada curtsied low, head bowed in reverence. When she lifted her head, she meet the prince's dark eyes. She read in them despair and worry and concern. Though the prince's front was strong, Ada sensed his need for a true friend, a true God.

"Ada, how's my mother? I haven't seen her in weeks. I'm worried about her."

"She's well, your Majesty. A little weary and nervous, but unharmed. Thank you for asking about her."

The prince opened his mouth as if he wanted to say more, but Panhsj placed a hand on Rameses's shoulder. "My Lord, your father requested your presence in the throne room immediately. I don't think we should keep him waiting."

Ada and Rameses both nodded and exchanged a wordless but knowing look. They both knew that the pharaoh was not in a good mood and was easily angered.

"Of course," Rameses said with a slight sigh. "Good-day, Ada." The prince and his bodyguards swept away into the darkness as Ada continued down the hallway.

Finally, up ahead, Ada saw a tiny gleam of light. She almost instantly found herself up against a wooden door and opened it. The door led into the kitchen. There were torches all about the kitchen, giving it some light, but even here it was still dark and the air thick. Tehara and an Israelite slave named Abalene were cooking some type of meat.

"Finally someone had the courage to come out in this blackness," Tehara mumbled, irritated.

"I came to get some refreshment for the queen," Ada explained for her sudden appearance. "Do you have anything that I can take to her?"

"Yes, we have just finished cooking some duck, and we have some bread and a bit of fruit left. Abalene, go get the bread from the pantry," Tehara ordered.

"Yes ma'am," Abalene replied meekly.

She was back in a moment with a reed basket. In it were a few pieces of bread and some figs. Tehara added the duck to the basket and handed it to Ada.

"Thank you very much," Ada said. She left the kitchen, closing the door behind her before she endeavored to make her way back through the blackness.

To her surprise, as she walked down one corridor she saw a light coming in her direction. She drew in her breath and tried to flatten herself against the wall, hoping that she would not be seen. Her heart was pumping as fear seeped back into her body. Her chest tightened. She tried to still her heavy breathing, but to no avail. Ada also realized that there was not enough room in the hallway for whoever it was to get past her, and that they had probably already seen her lamp. Quickly, she decided to just talk to the person outright and find out who it was.

"Who's there?" Ada asked, a slight tremble in her voice.

"Ada?" a voice questioned in surprise. Ada exhaled in relief, for by now she knew that voice well. It was the voice of Paki, her fiancé.

"Oh, thank goodness," Ada whispered.

"What're you doing here alone?" Paki demanded, coming up closer so that his light reflected off of her face.

"I came to get some food for the queen," Ada replied.

"Why didn't you ask me to go with you?" Paki persisted. "You know it's not safe for you to be by yourself in the palace, especially under these circumstances."

"I didn't know where you were," Ada murmured. "I'm sorry."

"It's all right," Paki replied, relaxing somewhat. "I'm just glad you didn't get hurt. But you must remember that I need to be with you if you have to go anywhere. The queen has ordered me to accompany you at all times."

"I will try," Ada promised. Then she added, "But I know that Yahweh will protect me. He controls whether I live or die."

There was a cold silence. Then Paki suggested, a little roughly, "Let's head back." He took Ada's lamp and held his torch and the lamp out in front of them.

For a while, silence reigned. Ada was still not quite comfortable with this pagan. He was a good friend to her, but nothing more. Though he was definitely kind and generous to everyone, Ada knew that he was a pagan, sacrificing to the Egyptian statues and paying no heed to Yahweh. If Ada had to be married to an Egyptian, there was no other one that she would prefer. But this man was nothing compared to Eitan, and Ada knew that she would never be able to truly love this man the way she should love a husband.

No matter how hard Ada tried to keep her thoughts and desire to love centered around Paki, it seemed that she could never stop thinking about Eitan. She had hoped that someday they would be able to marry. Now, that wasn't even a possibility. Eitan had all the character qualities she had always wished for in a husband, and he believed in Yahweh. Paki barely had half of those character qualities, and he didn't honor Yahweh in the least.

"Ada," Paki broke her train of thought, "it bothers me that you put so much confidence in your invisible God. You say that He will protect you, but that gives you no reason to put yourself into danger."

"I don't try to put myself into any unnecessary danger. I just said that my God controls whether I live or die. He has a plan and a purpose for my life, and nothing can happen to me but what He allows," Ada replied confidently.

"But how? How can a God that you cannot even see control you? How can He be powerful and how can you know Him when you can't even see Him?" Paki argued.

"Well, right now you can't see your gods, and they don't appear to be much help to you in these circumstances," Ada retorted, gently. "Egypt became a great nation because Yahweh blessed this land by Abraham's descendant, Joseph. Your Pharaoh doesn't even acknowledge Joseph—the one who Yahweh used to save your people from the great famine and bring all of Egypt under the pharaohs' control. He has hardened his heart against Yahweh and Yahweh's people. And if I ever doubted that He is true, all of these plagues have shown me that He really cares for us and that He really does exist."

"How many times do I have to tell you this?" Paki exclaimed, exasperatedly. "Ada, it's not your God, but *our* gods who are angry with us. It's our gods who are trying to show us something, but Pharaoh doesn't know what it is. Ada, I love you, but you must learn to love and trust our gods. It will be hard on our marriage when we believe in two different things."

"I cannot, Paki," Ada said quietly, but firmly.

"Why?" Paki questioned defensively.

"Because we—people—are made in Yahweh's image. Just look at the gods you have made. Most of them look like sick combinations of man and other creatures the true God has made. Snakes are sacred to you. We know that the serpent who caused the fall of our father Adam has been trying to displace Yahweh since the beginning of time. You raise up Pharaoh—a man—as if he is a god. But you say yourself that it's his behavior that's keeping the gods from being appeased. You are all so confused! Yahweh cannot be manipulated. He does what He pleases, and He has been patient with you because of His lovingkindness. But He told our father Abraham that He would bring his descendants back to the land He had shown to him, and there's nothing your gods, or Pharaoh, can do to stop Him because He is almighty. He controls the wind, the rain, the weather, and all parts of this earth. He is real, true, and just. There is no other god. I cannot deny Him.

"I don't know if I'll be one of the Israelites that Yahweh brings back to the Promised Land. He has His own purposes and He does not answer to me. But I know that He's the true God and is good and just. Perhaps He will leave me in Egypt to help you and the other Egyptians understand who He truly is. I'm at peace with my Maker, and whatever He tells me to do, I will do. Why don't you try trusting in Yahweh? Then maybe you will see and understand why I have such peace and confidence in my 'invisible' God."

Paki was silent. Ada knew that he had nothing more to say to defend his beliefs. She also realized that what she had said had been very bold—maybe too bold. If the pharaoh came to know about what she had just been sharing with Paki, she could be killed. Ada gulped, hoping, praying that Paki would respond well and not report her to Pharaoh.

"I'm sorry for becoming angry at you, Ada. I'll consider what you've said about your God," Paki responded, quietly.

Ada's heart leapt for joy. His heart was softening. She could tell that there was a tone in Paki's voice that she had never heard before. Maybe Yahweh wanted her here so that she could lead Paki to a love and knowledge of Him.

"Here you are," Paki said as his hand turned the handle of the door between two guards leading into the queen's chambers. Ada thanked him gratefully for escorting her.

"It was nothing," he said with a smile. "It's a good thing I know my way around so well, especially during this time of darkness. I'm just glad I'm able to run errands for people." Paki headed off in another direction as Ada entered the queen's apartment.

Torches and lamps hung all about the richly furnished room, but as in all the other rooms it was still dark and the air hung thickly. Lexine and an Egyptian maid by the name of Moselle sat in a corner doing the little mending that could be done in such dim light. The queen lay stretched out on her cushioned bed, restless and uneasy. The queen always liked to have something to do; whether it was ordering her servants around, making sure everything was flowing smoothly in the palace, visiting other royalty and nobility, or going down to the Nile to see what things were being imported from other countries. The queen hated being locked up in her room and wished there was something she could do to amuse herself.

"Here, my Queen. I've brought you some bread and meat." Ada set the basket by the queen's side and took out the delicacies.

"Thank you, Ada." The queen smiled with pleasure. "You are a constant source of happiness to me. I don't know what I would do if you weren't here. Being cramped up here is torture." The queen lifted the water to her lips.

Ada felt a twinge of sadness. The queen was so attached to her. If they were to ever be free, Ada felt sure that she would be kept in Egypt to serve the queen and be married to Paki. But what other choice did she have?

The queen ate in silence. Ada sat by her side, her hands folded calmly in her lap, thinking over the events of the last few days. The queen didn't finish all of her food and spoke to Ada, "Now you and the others should eat something, too, to keep up your strength."

Ada divided the food between the two other maids and herself, and when the meal was over they all felt satisfied.

Ada went back to the queen's side and the queen, leisurely propping herself up against her pillows, commanded, "Talk to me, Ada. I want something to entertain me. It's terrible not being able to do anything but sit here in this blackness."

"What would you like to hear about, my Queen?" Ada asked, ready to gratify the request.

There was a pause and then the queen spoke, almost tentatively, "Tell me some more about your God. It is very obvious to everyone in the palace that you possess a sort of peace that none of us have in this time of trial. Is it your God who gives you this peace, this tranquility?"

Ada's face lit up with joy. The queen rarely mentioned Yahweh. In fact, she hadn't allowed Ada to even mention Yahweh for over a month now. Maybe her heart was being softened just like Paki's.

"Yes, my Queen. I do believe that the real reason I'm at peace is because I have given the God of the Hebrews' my life. Whenever I give my all to Him, I know that I'm making Him happy. And I feel happier in return. Yahweh has blessed me and protected me thus far, and I know that it's because I've trusted Him completely, not just with what happens around me, but with my very life."

"And that's why you don't seem very worried about this darkness, or about the danger that surrounds you from the other Egyptian servants here?"

Ada nodded her head. "Yes, my lady."

The Queen sighed remorsefully. "I wish I could have such peace and confidence in our gods as you seem to have in yours. Our gods never give me peace or joy. Sometimes they even frighten me. I'm not quite sure what to do. It seems that we can never appease them. But tell me this: is it your God or our gods who are causing all these plagues and troubles to come upon us?"

"Well, my mistress, I believe that it's our God that is sending all of these troubles. We know how majestic and powerful He is, and we have been praying to Him for help and deliverance. I believe that He is finally answering our prayers. It would seem that He is afflicting your people because you will not let us go."

"You mean *my husband* will not let you go." the queen interrupted sharply. "Oh, there are many Egyptians who would very willingly send your people away. They have been advising my husband to send your nation away for quite some time. And does he listen? No."

"Would you like him to send us away, if it's Yahweh who's causing all of these trials?" Ada questioned.

"Well, I'm not sure, really. I would like to keep you and your nation here, but I believe that my husband has been wrong in treating your people so terribly. I wish that you could just live here and run your own lives like your people used to in the olden days. But if the only way to please your God is to let your nation go, I don't see that we have any other choice." The queen lapsed into silence, contemplating what to do.

For a while, Ada didn't know what to say. She finally ventured, hopefully, "Would you like me to tell you some more about Yahweh?"

"No, no. Not now," the queen said, absently. She seemed to be thinking hard.

The queen lay still for several minutes. Then she quickly sat up and commanded, "Ada, go get my finest dress and crown and get out my most ornamental wig and make-up."

"Yes, my Queen." Ada got up quickly to obey, but her face held a puzzled expression.

"I am going to see my husband," the queen said determinedly, answering Ada's silent question. "If your God really does answer prayers, you should say one to Him right now. I'm going to beg Pharaoh to let your people go."

ב

"Knock knock," Jarah called cheerfully. She peered into Amissa's open doorway and was quite pleased to see her friend propped up into a sitting position with some coarse woolen blankets. Ezra sat by his sister's side, holding her hand gently. Amissa's eyes brightened at the sight of Jarah. She smiled and Jarah was relieved to see that the color had returned to her friend's cheeks.

"Come in," Amissa said eagerly. Ezra rose from the stool and offered it to Jarah. She nodded at him and took the vacated seat. Ezra headed out the back door towards a small shade tree.

"How are you feeling?" Jarah asked.

"Much better, thank you. The fever broke this morning. I suppose that I will be up and about in just a few days," Amissa replied with a small grin.

"I'm so glad," Jarah exclaimed in earnest. "Here, I made this for you." Jarah produced a hidden sweet bread from the basket she had brought along. "I know this is your favorite."

"Oh, how did you know?" Amissa asked breathlessly. She smelled the sweet, sticky scent and sighed contentedly. "Now there's nothing that could make my day better, except—" Amissa paused abruptly.

"Except what?" Jarah prodded. Amissa's eyes glazed over with tears and she focused her gaze on the dirt floor. "It's Ada, isn't it?" Jarah answered for her friend.

"Yes. We haven't heard anything from her, and it's been five days," Amissa said between sobs. She swallowed hard, still averting Jarah's gaze.

"I'm sure she'll be all right," Jarah soothed, patting her friend's cool hand. But even she didn't feel convinced.

"Has your father done anything to try and locate her?"

Both the girls started at the sudden question. Eitan was standing right behind Jarah's shoulder. He must have come in unobserved by the two girls, and had overheard their conversation. Amissa shrugged her shoulders and brushed a stray strand of hair back from her forehead.

"Father says it would be hopeless. We would never be able to find our way into the palace, much less locate Ada." Amissa released the tension from her shoulders and tried to regain her composure. She inhaled deeply, and then smiled weakly up at Eitan.

"Is her life in great danger?" Urgency rose in Eitan's voice.

"I—I hope not. Father and Ezra are concerned, but they don't seem to be too worried. Paki and the queen are protecting her, and Yahweh knows that she's there, too." There was a long pause. Everyone's thoughts were focused on Ada, wondering if she was still alive. No one knew what was happening in the darkness, or what Ada was doing.

Just then some sweet, lively strains of music floated into the house. *Ezra's flute.* As that thought crossed Jarah's mind, she felt a calming peace flood over her. Amissa appeared to feel it, too, and she seemed to be relaxing.

"Is there anything I can do for Ada?" Eitan asked, though the question didn't seem to be pointed to anyone in particular.

"No." Amissa drew a long breath. "Only Yahweh can help her now." Amissa looked deeply into Jarah's eyes and then squeezed her hand.

"I'm sure Yahweh is watching out for her and that you'll hear from Ada very soon," Jarah assured her friend, in a much more forceful tone than she felt.

"I hope you're right," Amissa replied, doubt foremost in her tone and look.

"Jarah, we need to go back home. Mother needs us," Eitan said. "I'm glad you're feeling better, Amissa."

"Thank you, Eitan. And thank you, Jarah, for your quick visit. You have encouraged me more than you'll ever know. Oh, and Eitan? Thank you for carrying me when I didn't have the strength to stand." Amissa lowered her eyes, ashamed.

Eitan nodded slightly, "You're welcome," he murmured.

"I'm glad we were a blessing to you," Jarah said with a forced smile. She gave Amissa's hand one more gentle squeeze then left the house with Eitan. His countenance was dark, as if overshadowed by a cloud. *He's worried about Ada*, Jarah thought, *and he probably should be.* Then she prayed silently, *Yahweh, please protect Ada, and help her family have peace in You.*

BEFORE THE PHARAOH

The queen walked with strong, purposeful steps through the palace halls, yet in her heart she felt trepidation. Two Egyptian guards followed behind her and one walked ahead with a blazing torch in his hand. Only their soft footsteps could be heard as the party made their way through the massive palace.

Finally, they reached the throne room, and the queen turned to the guards and instructed them, "Wait here for my return." She brushed back her hair, smoothed her dress, and laid her hands on the door. Though she was nervous about this encounter with her husband, she was not going to turn back now or show her emotions. She pushed the doors open and lifted up her chin as she walked with dignity into the throne room. The doors creaked and groaned as they swung open on their hinges and then closed with a resounding bang.

Instantly four guards jumped forward and raised a torch to see who it was. There were exclamations of surprise as they jumped back and one guard said apologetically, "We're most sorry, my Queen. Please, enter."

The queen stepped forward into the large, open space. On the walls, flames of light danced and made a dim glow. In the far left corner several magicians sat poring over their books and spells. Guards and sentries lined the walls and several servants walked to and fro, bringing food for the magicians and the pharaoh. Pharaoh himself sat on a dais at the far end of the hall, talking with… their son. Pharaoh's gold throne glowed eerily in the torchlight as he looked up in surprise. The queen approached the dais and bowed low, locking eyes with her son for a brief moment. He was smiling, happy to see her.

"My Lady," the pharaoh exclaimed, "what is it you wish of me? Has something happened to you? Is there a problem in the palace?" Pharaoh was a little alarmed, for his queen didn't usually come to see him of her own free will. Both of them were very strong-willed and their personalities and opinions often clashed.

"No, my Lord, everything is well with me. It's about the Hebrew nation that I have come to speak to you," the queen replied.

"Oh?" Pharaoh asked, his curiosity very much aroused.

"My Lord and my King, I have been talking with one of my Hebrew maids and she believes that it's not our gods who are bringing on all this trouble, but their God. It would seem that until you allow these people to go to their own land we will have no end of trials here in Egypt. Please, my Lord, reconsider keeping these people as slaves. I'm sure that you, as much as I, would wish that our land be left in peace."

During the queen's appeal, the pharaoh's handsome and strong face had grown darker and darker. The prince's face had grown pale and sad. The queen bit her lip, realizing that her plea was in vain.

With a scowl, Pharaoh answered her in a tone of anger, "I wouldn't have thought it of you, my Queen, to ask for their freedom. I've made my decision, and it is final. Nothing can make me let the Israelite nation go. Don't you see how much good they have done us? Our Egyptian nation has grown mighty and strong, and without them we will never be able to rebuild our lives, or our foreign status."

"But if we keep them, their God will utterly destroy us," the queen exclaimed.

"Enough," her husband roared. "I've made my decision, and I cannot be moved from it. I will prove that I am more powerful than the God of the Israelites. Now go!" and with a wave of his hand, he dismissed the queen.

The queen peered at her son. His head was down in a despairing way. He slowly lifted his head, staring into her eyes. She knew that Rameses felt the way she did. But she knew that there was nothing more either of them could do to change the pharaoh's mind. Wrenching her eyes from her son's face, she turned away reluctantly. If what Ada said was true, then Egypt would be left as nothing by the time Pharaoh's heart was changed. Suddenly she turned back to the pharaoh and said, "I'm not sure why I believe what my maid says, but I really feel and believe that because of your hard heart, utter destruction will be brought onto our nation. I cannot say anything to change your mind, so I will not endeavor to. But because you have not listened, you will now see the consequences."

"I told you to leave my presence!" Pharaoh shouted, gesturing angrily at her. The prince recoiled in fear. The queen stiffened, feeling Pharaoh's anger and resentment.

"Yes, my King," the queen replied, bowing, and then exited through the wooden doors. She had done all she could possibly do to save her husband, her son, and her nation. Now the fate of the Egyptian people lay in the hands of the Israelite's God.

א

A few days later, Pharaoh begged Moses to get rid of the darkness. Moses prayed to Yahweh and the darkness was lifted from Egypt. But once again, the Israelites were forced into the vile service of Pharaoh. All of the Hebrews hoped that it wouldn't be long before Yahweh again gave heed to their cries for deliverance.

THE PASSOVER

Not too long after they had started work again, Moses called all the leaders of Israel together and told them something of great importance. Jarah listened attentively as her father told them the following instructions:

"Tomorrow we have to take a one-year-old male goat or sheep and kill it. Then we must spread the blood on the doorposts of our house and cook the lamb over an open fire. We must eat the lamb with bitter herbs and unleavened bread and be ready to leave in a moments' notice. This meal is to be called 'The Passover.' I know that these may sound like very strange instructions, but by this time I think we all know better than to disobey Yahweh," Father stated.

"Also," Eitan said, continuing where his father had left off, "Moses and Aaron said that if anyone doesn't follow Yahweh's instructions and put the blood on their doorposts that their family won't be saved from a terrible plague that's going to pass through the land. This plague will be the worst one yet. Yahweh's angel is going to come down and strike every firstborn male in each household among the Egyptians and their cattle. The blood on the door will be a marker of which houses belong to the Israelites, and the Angel of Death will not enter those homes."

Everyone was silent as they contemplated the severity of the coming plague. Jarah began to feel nervous. *What if we don't do all of the instructions right? What will happen then? Will Eitan die?* These questions voiced themselves over and over again in Jarah's mind. She tried to assure herself that everything would be fine, but Jarah had jittery feelings for the rest of that day, and all of the next.

The next afternoon, Jarah and Lemuel went to their herd of sheep and goats to try to find an animal perfect for the sacrifice. Fruitlessly they tried to find one without a spot on it.

Finally Lemuel pointed to a smaller lamb and said, "This one's a year old."

It was pure white and so little and cute that Jarah could not help but wish it didn't have to be that lamb, of all the lambs they owned. Lemuel gave a small sigh. Jarah then realized that it was the lamb whose mother had died and Lemuel had nursed the lamb back to health all by himself. It was a special lamb to Lemuel and he loved it very much. While Jarah thought about this, she looked around at the rest of their lambs and baby goats. No other one was absolutely perfect. The lamb looked up at her and gave a little "Baaaaa!"

"That's the only one that's perfect, Lemuel," Jarah uttered quietly with a long, drawn out sigh.

Lemuel knew that she was right, but his eyes were moist with tears as he bent down and gathered the little fleecy ball into his arms. They didn't speak as they walked on the narrow shepherd's path back towards their house. They were too busy with thoughts of what was about to happen to the lamb and what would happen that night.

As they turned the corner and neared their home, they saw that their father had started a fire. Some hyssop reeds lay at his feet. They were for spreading the blood on the doorpost. Lemuel approached him, almost hesitantly, and handed over the lamb.

"It's a beautiful lamb, Lemuel, and I'm thankful you were willing to sacrifice it for the protection of our family."

The Passover

Father smiled kindly at Lemuel and pulled a sharp, pointed dagger from his tunic. Jarah covered her eyes and ran into the house, fighting back stinging tears.

Upon entering their dwelling, the sickening smell of the bitter herbs being boiled greeted her.

"Jarah, please help Tirzah pack up the clothes. Eitan? Finish taking out those bundles and putting them on the cart. You're just standing around doing nothing. Be useful. Oh, and make sure that the donkeys and oxen are well watered," Mother called after Eitan as he left the door. "Shayna, don't let the herbs boil too long, and take down the curtains from the windows. Jarah can put them in with the rest of the clothes. Once the windows are uncovered it will at least get some of the smell out of this room. Raphael, set the table with those dishes and give the rest that we aren't using to Tirzah. Hurry up girls. Dusk is coming on quickly."

As their mother continued to hand out orders right and left there was a great scurrying around the hut. Eitan took out the packed bundles as quickly as the girls packed them. Raphael ran around the table putting out the dishes with one hand and holding his nose with the other to keep out the nauseating scent.

"Jarah, let Tirzah and Eitan finish with the bundles. Help bake the bread," Mother commanded as she bustled outside to check on how the lamb was cooking.

A few minutes later, everything—except what they would use that night—was packed and the meal was ready to be eaten. Father and Lemuel came inside with the cooked lamb. Lemuel had a hurt look in his eyes as he joined the rest of the family at the table.

Poor Lemuel, Jarah thought mournfully, exchanging a cheerless smile with him.

Father said a prayer over the food and they ate the meal in silence, standing up and ready for whatever was going to happen. The food tasted much better than it smelled, but Jarah couldn't keep her eyes from Lemuel's sad face as he picked at his food.

The meal was finished as twilight came. Nothing had happened. Father, Eitan, and Lemuel went outside to extinguish the fire and clean up the blood that had fallen to the ground. The doorpost was thoroughly painted, but Jarah still felt uneasy as she and Shayna packed up the last of the washed dishes. The little boys were already in bed, and outside nothing else made a sound. Lamps were lit in all the nearby windows and oxen and donkeys grazed close to the houses all throughout Goshen. The silence was almost suffocating. Outside the night sky appeared normal. The stars twinkled on the horizon and the rainbow of colors in the western expanse showed that the sun had just set.

What will happen tonight? Jarah worried. She looked towards Eitan. *He seems normal. He doesn't appear worried about what might happen. Neither does Father. Mother does a little, but not much. I guess I shouldn't fret, either.*

Everyone retired early that night, except for Jarah and Mother. Jarah stood in the open doorway, looking up at the stars.

"Jarah, it's time to rest now." Her mother's voice sounded coarse and weak, telling Jarah that she was anxious and nervous.

"Yes, Mother," Jarah acknowledged absently. But she didn't move. She leaned against the doorpost, her eyes focusing on one lone, bright star. She had looked at it several times before, but tonight it seemed special. She had a hard time pulling her eyes away from it.

Finally, she mustered up the will to walk away from the night air and cautiously crawl into her bed so as not to wake Tirzah. Though she tossed and turned for quite some time, Jarah eventually fell into a fitful sleep.

א

Jarah felt a slight wind gently stroking her face. She started and opened her eyes. The room was quite dark, showing that it was still the middle of the night. Everyone else was sleeping soundly. Jarah glanced over at Eitan's bed. He was breathing evenly and looked very peaceful.

I wonder if the plague has come yet. I hope it has, Jarah thought uneasily. She lay down, but suddenly she heard a slight rustle outside. Was it the wind, or was it someone's garments? She couldn't tell. Abruptly someone, or something, came into the house.

The Passover

It was a shining man, taller than Father or Eitan, with robes of shimmering silver. How he had entered Jarah didn't know unless he had somehow entered through the closed door. His angry eyes were filled with one purpose, and he stared at only one thing in the house. The man slid quickly across the room and approached Eitan's bed. Jarah drew in her breath as the man drew a flaming sword and extended it above Eitan's body as if to strike him a heavy blow. Jarah screamed, "Eitan!" but Eitan didn't move as the huge, shining blade shot down towards Eitan's body.

"Eitan, look out!" Jarah shouted as it came closer and closer to her brother, but Eitan didn't hear her and before Jarah could do anything else, it was too late...

ב

Jarah sat up in bed, gasping for air and drenched with sweat. *What? What happened?* Jarah turned and looked around the hut. Everyone was asleep and unmoved. Jarah climbed silently out of her bed and ran over to where Eitan slept. He was breathing deep, regular breaths, a small, peaceful smile on his lips. Jarah sighed in utter relief. *It was only a nightmare,* she told herself, reassuringly.

She slowly crossed the room and gently climbed back into bed. Despite being nervous about the dream, Jarah was so exhausted that she soon drifted back to sleep.

ג

Paki sat up in bed. He could feel a tingling sensation in his bones. He had felt a panicky feeling in the pit of his stomach all day. He had tried not to reveal it to anyone, especially his family members, but now it was almost unbearable. He slipped out of bed very quietly so as not to wake his nine-year-old brother, Jahi, who slept besides him.

Paki went out of the bedroom and passed the rooms where his parents and younger sisters, Ife and Keket, slept peacefully. He couldn't help but smile affectionately at Ife, his thirteen-year-old sister, as she cuddled closer to Keket. Keket absolutely adored Paki, and he gladly returned her childish affection. At only six years old, she still loved to be hugged and played with.

Paki paced about the house, the pale moonlight bathing him in its light. Vainly he tried to relax, but he continued to feel more and more awake and anxious with each step.

"Paki, is there something wrong?" Paki's mother, Hathor, suddenly stood by his shoulder.

"I just couldn't sleep," Paki admitted. "What are you doing up?"

"I couldn't sleep, either. You look very troubled. Are you sure nothing's wrong? Is it something with the queen, or with Ada?" his mother probed.

"Well, Ada did tell me something today. It seems like all of the Israelites believe that another plague is coming, one worse than all the plagues before. They have to eat specially prepared food and paint blood on the doorposts to protect themselves from the plague. She said that if I wanted to live our family should do the same. She was pleading with me—crying, actually. She said I was going to die. I told her I didn't believe in her God and that I wasn't going to do what she said. But Ada seemed so worried, so sad and concerned. That's what I've been thinking about."

"Don't worry about that any more. All of the Hebrews have strange customs and there's no reason why we should adopt them. I'm sure there can be nothing more severe than any of the plagues that have already happened to us. We just brought a sacrifice to the temple of Ra yesterday, so I'm sure his protection will be on our family. There's nothing to fret about, so go back to sleep," Hathor soothed.

"Yes, Mother. I'll try," Paki began. He smiled half-heartedly at his mother, embraced her lightly, and turned on his heel to go back to his room. Climbing back into bed, he tried to sleep.

The next thing Paki knew his heart began to pound in his ears and pain shot up and down his body. His body began to convulse and he couldn't breathe. But just as quickly as the convulsions started, they stopped again, and Paki's body lay still.

Jahi sat up quickly in bed. His brother's sudden movements had startled him out of a deep sleep.

The Passover

"Paki? What's wrong? Jahi asked, looking over at his brother. Paki didn't move. "Paki?" Jahi questioned again, shaking his brother gently. There was still no response.

Jahi ran from the room and nearly bumped into his mother, who was heading back to her own bed.

"Mother," he faltered.

"Yes, dear. What is it?" his mother asked, slightly impatient that he was up so late in the night.

"Paki—he won't wake up," Jahi replied.

"He won't wake up? What are you talking about?" Hathor exclaimed, suddenly focusing all of her attention on her young son.

"He won't open his eyes. Come look," Jahi explained and pulled his mother towards the bedroom. On the table besides Hathor a lamp was burning. She grabbed it and rushed after Jahi, holding the lamp over Paki's body. Paki's face was an ashen color and he didn't respond to his mother's firm touch on the shoulder.

"Ammon," Hathor screamed.

In a moment Ammon was at his wife's side, seeing what was wrong with Paki.

"Mother, what's wrong?" Ife asked, bringing the trembling Keket with her.

"Will Paki be all right?" Keket asked, clinging to her mother in terror, staring at her brother's pale face.

"Please, Paki. Please wake up," Jahi pleaded.

As Ife saw her brother's white face, she whispered, "Is he—" but could not finish the sentence.

"What is it? What's wrong?" Keket practically screamed.

Ammon looked up at his wife, tears gathering in his eyes as he answered Keket's question in a quivering tone, "Paki has... He's— He's dead."

א

Acenith collapsed on the floor, crying and heartbroken. Her brother, her dearest friend, her only companion, was dead. Her father, drunken and enraged, stood over the form of his lifeless son.

Acenith knew that Bes was her father's only pride and joy. Now there was nothing left for him or her. Her father suddenly broke out into foul, angry curses. Acenith crumpled even lower to the floor and covered her ears, sobbing uncontrollably.

"You, you did this!" her father roared.

"No, Father. I didn't. Why would I? I love Bes. Please, Father. I did nothing!" Acenith screamed.

But her drunk, angry father wasn't listening to her. He attacked her, punching her with his fists. Acenith screamed and tried to run away, but her father shoved her into a chair and continue to beat her.

"Please Father, stop! Please," Acenith shouted, trying unsuccessfully to block his blows. She finally ducked under his arms but he grabbed her and flung her out into the street.

"Get out of here and never come back," he yelled at her, slamming the door behind her.

Acenith, broken, bruised, and bleeding, ran frantically away into the night. She didn't know where to go or what to do. She knew no one who would help her. Everyone she knew was like her father—cold and ruthless. She knew she would never be able to return to him. But even though he had often mistreated and abused her, Acenith knew as she fled through the night that she had left half of her heart with her father. The other half of her heart rested in the bosom of her dead brother.

ה

Ada was awakened abruptly by the sound of a scream from inside the palace. Instantly she was out of bed and running towards the door.

"Ada? What's wrong?" Lexine asked.

"I heard the queen scream. We must go and help her. Something could be terribly wrong." Ada fumbled in the dark for the door.

"Are you sure it was her?" Lexine asked, though she was already throwing a shawl around her shoulders.

"Yes, I'm sure of it. I would know her scream anywhere," Ada responded urgently.

The Passover

The two servants ran down the hallway towards the queen's room. It was empty. The door was open and the bed-clothes were thrown back. The soldiers who guarded the queen's room were no where in sight.

"Where is she?"

Ada was about to answer when she suddenly heard loud wailing from farther down the corridor.

"That's her. Quickly, follow me," Ada instructed.

The lamentations were coming from the prince's chambers. The door was wide open and two soldiers stood close by, talking in low, somber tones. They let Ada and Lexine into the room without hesitation, knowing on what errand they had come.

The queen was kneeling next to Rameses, screaming, wailing, and wringing her hands in grief. A magician was by the prince's side and Pharaoh stood a few paces away.

"No, come back. Please. Don't let him be dead!" the queen shrieked.

The magician stood up and looked sadly at the Pharaoh.

"I'm sorry, but there's nothing else I can do."

"NO!" the queen wailed again, kissing the dead prince's face and sobbing bitterly.

The sounds of more wailing from other houses and rooms began to fill the city. More and more people were discovering that their own sons were also dead. Ada walked up to the queen, trying to comfort her, but the queen refused to be consoled.

Pharaoh stood as still as a statue but tears coursed down his own hardened face. The pharaoh had never imagined anything like this would happen. He had been warned, but he had not listened. Now he could not take back his actions. In the hardness of his heart, he had killed his own son.

Ada sighed sadly, knowing that Yahweh's wrath had finally been appeased. *It is finished,* she told herself. *Yahweh was merciful to them as long as was possible. But even though each of the plagues attacked the Egyptians' gods and showed that they were powerless, the people didn't listen. It's only by His grace that Yahweh killed just the firstborn males. Yahweh's work is done, and He has finally avenged his people. All of the Hebrew boys who the previous Pharaohs murdered have finally been paid for in the blood of the first born Egyptian males. If only Pharaoh hadn't continued in hardness of heart against our people and remembered all that we've done for him and how our father Joseph saved his nation. I can only pray that now the Egyptians will finally repent and maybe I can be of some help to the queen.*

THE PROMISED LAND

As Jarah woke up the next morning, she felt that something wonderful had happened. She jumped out of bed and looked around. Mother was up, packing a box. Lemuel was awake, too, fixing a leg on one of the stools. Shayna was mending a dress. Raphael and Yanni were sound asleep and Tirzah was slowly waking up. Bright yellow sunlight was streaming in through the windows.

"Where's Father and Eitan?" Jarah asked,

"Shush. Keep your voice down," Mother hissed. "They went to the meeting of the elders."

"And now we're back," Father and Eitan strode into the house. They were both beaming.

"What happened? What happened?" Jarah cried, running up to her father.

Father looked around the hut at the expectant faces. He reached out, grabbed Jarah's hand, and squeezed it. Looking right into her eyes he said, "Yahweh has answered our prayers. We are free."

"What?" Jarah, Lemuel, and Tirzah gasped out at the same time.

"We are *free!*" Father shouted, jubilant.

Jarah screamed and jumped up and down. Shayna stood as if rooted to the floor, her jaw hanging open. Lemuel and Eitan embraced. Father ran up to Mother and kissed her cheek. She blushed, laughed, and swatted him away, playfully.

"I can't believe it! I can't believe it!" Jarah exclaimed, laughing and crying at the same time. Lemuel grabbed Jarah and swung her around.

"Believe it," he told her, laughing.

"What's going on?" Raphael asked groggily, rubbing his eyes.

"Pharaoh has freed us. We're going to the Promised Land!" Father said, pulling his little son out of bed and putting him on his shoulder. Yanni crawled out of bed and ran around the house shrieking with joy, even though he didn't know why everyone was so excited.

"Now everyone, quiet down and listen," Father shouted above the hubbub. "We must thank Yahweh, and we must also pray for the Egyptians. The plague did indeed come last night." Father paused for a moment and took a deep breath. A tear glistened in his eye. "All the firstborn males in Egypt are dead."

A stunned silence rested in the room.

"We must pray for their comfort, that they will be drawn to Yahweh, and that Yahweh will bless the Egyptian nation and restore them," Father finished, sorrow evident on his face.

"Father, after all the Egyptians have done to us? You want us to pray for *them*? Aren't they getting what they richly deserve?" Shayna asked, a hint of smugness in her voice.

"Shayna, we should never, ever be happy about death, and especially not the destruction of an entire nation, no matter what they've done to anyone. Be thankful that we haven't gotten what we richly deserve. Yahweh has shown us mercy. We, too, deserve death because of our sin. But Yahweh has been gracious to us. Do you understand?" Father said, staring Shayna directly in the eyes.

Shayna shifted her weight and lowered her eyes, deflated. "Yes, Father."

Father knelt on the floor and motioned for everyone else to do the same. Jarah knelt next to her father, her heart bursting with excitement, joy, and yet sorrow for the Egyptians. She was surprised and happy to see that even though Mother didn't join them in prayer, Shayna bowed her head with the rest of the family.

When the family rose from their knees Father said, "Now we all need to eat and pack up quickly. Mariel, Moses gave us instructions to go ask the Egyptians for provisions for our journey. Can you ask some of the Egyptians that you've met for supplies?"

"Gladly," Mother said, a greedy glint in her eyes.

"But before we all move on with our tasks," Father began, "I have something I want to say." Father put his arm around Mother's shoulders. Mother was smiling. Mother rarely smiled.

"We wanted to tell you that your mother is pregnant. There's another baby on the way."

"Really?" Tirzah squealed.

"Really," Father said, grinning.

The children stood, frozen. Jarah was shocked. Then, she started laughing. She was so happy, so surprised. Her laughter seemed to jolt the family back to the present. Tirzah screamed and hugged her mother. Raphael and Yanni were talking over each other, asking, "What? A baby? When?" Shayna was beaming. Eitan looked at Jarah, grinning.

"You knew, didn't you?" Jarah exclaimed, playfully punching Eitan in the arm.

"Yes, I knew," Eitan replied, tweaking Jarah's nose.

"Why didn't you tell me?" Lemuel demanded, but he was grinning ear to ear.

"Because I just found out early this morning, Lem," Eitan stated, ruffling Lemuel's hair.

"All right, everyone. Let's get moving," Father shouted over the conversation, clapping his hands for emphasis.

Mother hurried off to get gold, jewels, and food for their journey. According to Moses' instructions, all the food left over from last night's dinner had been burned. Shayna, Jarah, and Tirzah packed up the bed clothes and kitchen utensils. Father and Lemuel took Raphael and Yanni outside to take care of the animals and finish picking the vegetables from their garden. Eitan was loading boxes onto the cart.

The street was filled with shouts of joy and exaltation. Instruments were playing; cymbals and tambourines were adding their notes to the songs. People were singing and dancing as they moved about, greeting their friends and family members and packing up to leave this terrible place of oppression forever. Even the sheep, goats, and donkeys seemed to be kicking up their heels in delight. The cows added their low notes to the high notes of reeds and pipes as more and more people poured out of their houses to celebrate this glorious day. Jarah moved to the doorway and leaned against it, basking in the sun and looking on at the scene before her. Her heart was about to burst with joy. At last, they were leaving, forever.

"Jarah, come on out back. I need help," Shayna called. Jarah sighed happily and ran around the house.

"I don't care if Shayna's being bossy," she declared, giggling at the thought. "This is the best day of my life."

א

It was late morning when Ada smoothed her dress and knocked softly on the queen's bed chamber door. She hoped the queen had cried herself to sleep, but a soft, tearful reply of "Come in," told Ada that her hopes were in vain.

"Ah Ada," the queen sighed as Ada presented herself before the dismantled queen. The queen had slept some that night, but her face was still stained with tears and her hair was unkempt. She sighed sorrowfully again and then whispered, "How can I ever thank you for how kind you have been to me?"

"No thanks are necessary, my Queen. You have always been so considerate of me. Why should I not return your love?"

"Yes, but I always wish I could have done more, and I wish I would have listened to you when you talked about that young man you wanted to marry..." the queen's voice faded away.

"Is Paki also—" Ada did not say the dreaded word. She gulped back tears.

"Yes. He, too, was taken, along with... all the others." The queen started sobbing. "I will miss my son," she whispered, looking up at Ada with tear-filled eyes. Ada put her arm around the queen comfortingly as the queen wept. It was many minutes before the queen regained her composure.

"Ada," she finally said, "I have decided to let you go with your people. I feel that if I were to keep you I would bring on the anger of your God. I wholly believe in Him now, Ada. I prayed to Him last night, and He has given me a taste of the peace that you have always told me about."

"Oh my Queen, I'm so happy for you," Ada exclaimed in delight.

"Yes. Thank you for telling me about Him, Ada. But you must go and get ready to go to your own land. You are one of Yahweh's chosen people, and I'm sure that He has a mighty plan for your life. Go, my child, with my blessing."

"Oh thank you, your Majesty. I shall miss you ever so much," Ada said, gratefully, rising from the bed.

"I will miss you, too," the queen whispered.

For a moment the two women stared at each other. Then the queen thrust all of her royal manners aside, jumped up, and hugged Ada close. Ada returned the embrace, sobbing slightly with the joy of being released and the sadness that this was the last time she would ever see the queen.

"Go my child, and may Yahweh bless you," the queen choked. She drew back and looked fondly at Ada, tears glittered in her eyes. She swallowed hard and then said, "I will send one of my guards with you and Lexine to escort you both back to your own families. And I will also give you many gifts as thanks for your service and your kindness."

Ada nodded, hardly trusting herself to speak. "Thank you, my queen. You are too kind."

The queen smiled and then said, "You must go or you won't be able to leave with your family. I'll have the guard at your door in a few minutes with your gifts."

Ada nodded, took one last look at her beautiful surroundings and the queen who had, in a strange way, become almost like a second mother to her. Then, she quietly left. She and Lexine packed up their few belongings in silence and then traveled with the guards through the palace and out to the street.

As they left the front entrance, Ada could not help but look back one last time. This palace had been her home for three years, and the queen and servants in it had been her friends and companions. Now she was leaving it and all its finery and starting a new life. The feeling was bittersweet, but as she stared out at the golden desert she knew that Yahweh would work everything for good. Though she still felt tears in her eyes, Ada knew that she would soon get over this sadness that she felt inside. Already she was beginning to feel a serene peace creeping over her. And as she thought about her family—and about Eitan—Ada knew that there was nothing else she would love to do more than leave for the Promised Land.

בּ

Jarah's family was dispersed among the neighbors and friends outside the house, finishing last minute details. Sitting in the back of the house with the wagon, Jarah talked with Amissa about her mother being pregnant when they heard voices inside the house.

"Eitan, may I speak with you, please?" It was Ada's voice!

"What's wrong, Ada?" Eitan asked. He sounded very kind and caring.

"Ada's back!" Amissa gasped.

"Why is she here? What's wrong with her? Does she get to come with us?" Jarah pondered aloud.

"I don't know," Amissa replied. Her face held a very confused look.

"It sounds like your father is there, too," Jarah said, cocking her head to the side so that she could listen. "I wonder what's going on."

"We shouldn't be listening behind the door," Amissa said, slowly moving away to pet the oxen, though it was obvious that she wanted to run inside and greet Ada. Jarah followed reluctantly. Amissa stroked the oxen's noses, thinking hard.

"I really hope Ada can go with us. That must be why she's here. But I thought she was betrothed to Paki and couldn't go." Then Amissa's eyes grew very big and she looked at Jarah with a stunned expression on her face.

"Jarah… Paki was a firstborn!" she said in a soft, awestruck whisper.

"Then do you think he's…?" Jarah whispered back, hardly daring to say what she thought. Suddenly, a terrible thought struck her. *Acenith! And Bes! I know many of the Egyptians were warned. Were they warned, too? Is Bes alive? Oh, I wish I knew what happened to them.* Amissa's voice broke into her thoughts.

"Paki, he must've, well, you know. That must be why Ada's back. But why would she and Father be talking to Eitan?"

Jarah's heart leapt inside of her. "I know," Jarah replied, proudly. "She's telling Eitan that she can marry him."

"What? When did Eitan ask her to marry him?" Amissa asked, incredulously.

Jarah explained everything to her and then added, "Eitan will be so happy. He really loves Ada and he was almost heartbroken when he heard about Paki."

"I should think so. I never knew he asked her!" exclaimed Amissa.

From around the side of the house Jarah's father called, "Jarah, it's time to get the cart out. Your mother is back with goods from the Egyptians and everyone's ready to go. Oh, your family is looking for you, Amissa."

"Yes sir. Thank you," Amissa said with a smile and hurried away.

Father pulled out the cart and Shayna put in two baskets that were filled to the brim with jewelry and clothing. Another pan was filled with dough for bread. Yanni and Raphael climbed into the cart with Tirzah. Eitan climbed up to take control of the oxen. Mother also clambered into the cart, settling back against the dry reeds that lined it for comfort. Shayna rode on another small donkey next to the cart to talk with Ada, for Eitan had invited Ada to sit with him in the front of the wagon. Ada had accepted Eitan's hand in marriage and they both looked so happy. They were practically glowing. Father was walking along besides the cart keeping things in order while Lemuel and Ezra drove the flocks of sheep and goats behind the carts of their two families. Jarah and Amissa rode on another donkey together.

As the whole procession started after the rest of the Israelites who were making their way out of Egypt with Moses and Aaron, Amissa leaned up to Jarah's ear and whispered in a teasing tone, "You're shaking. Are you crying or laughing?"

"I—I don't know. I think I'm doing both." The girls both laughed. "I'm sorry, I'm just so excited and so numb with shock and disbelief, I almost don't know how to react."

"Then sing like everyone else," Amissa suggested.

Above the hubbub of the trampling of feet and joyful laughter and the squawks of chickens and geese, there came the sound of female voices singing with tambourines and lyres:

> *"I will sing to the Lord,*
> *For He is highly exalted.*
> *The Lord is my strength and song,*
> *And He has become my salvation;*
> *This is my God, and I will praise Him;*
> *My Father's God, and I will extol Him.*
> *Your right hand, O Lord,*
> *Is majestic in power.*
> *Your left hand, O Lord,*
> *Shatters the enemy.*
> *Who is like You among gods, O Lord?*
> *Who is like You, majestic in holiness?*
> *Awesome in praises, working wonders?"*

And then Miriam's, Moses' sister, voice rose above the others in the chorus:

> *"Sing to the Lord, for He is highly exalted;*
> *Sing to the Lord, for He is highly exalted;*
> *In Your loving-kindness You have led the*
> *People whom you have redeemed;*

The Promised Land

*In Your strength You have guided them
To Your holy habitation.
Sing to the Lord!
Sing to the Lord!"*

The song continued to echo around Jarah. She sighed with happiness, her heart pounding with joy and excitement. She looked around and saw her family all together, happy. Even Mother was smiling and joyful. There was Amissa's family in the wagon next to them, singing, laughing, and joking. Jarah's eyes rested on Eitan and Ada, sitting close together at the front of the wagon. They were beaming. Jarah's face lit up in a smile as she thought, *Ada's free, too, free to marry Eitan and come with us.*

Even though Jarah was thrilled beyond belief to be leaving Egypt, she couldn't help but feel a tiny bit sad for the Egyptians. After all, they had lost so much. It would take them years to rebuild their nation. Then, she realized something.

But they can rebuild their nation. Yahweh's plagues didn't completely destroy them. He left many people alive. They will become great again. I didn't think about it before, but Yahweh really is merciful—to us, and to the Egyptians.

Then Jarah gasped a little. *Oh no. I forgot about Acenith. I should've gone to see her.* Jarah craned her neck backwards. Already the dark, forlorn city was growing small in the distance. There was no turning back now. Jarah felt her shoulders sagging. She was worried about her friend. *Did someone warn her about the plague? Did Bes live? And... Will I ever see Acenith again?*

"Jarah, what's wrong?" Amissa asked.

Jarah shook her head and tried to smile. "I was just thinking about one of my Egyptian friends. I wish I had been able to say good-bye to her."

"I'm sorry." Amissa laid a compassionate hand on Jarah's arm. "But you never know. Maybe she came with us. Mother said that a few Egyptians came with us because they believe in Yahweh. So maybe she's here and you can see her again."

"Maybe. I certainly hope so," Jarah said, wistfully.

Yahweh, please, help Acenith. And please... Can I see her again someday?

"Jarah, come on. Keep up," Lemuel shouted.

Jarah grinned. "Coming." She and Amissa laughed as they kicked the donkey into a trot. Jarah knew it wasn't time to be sad or worried. Yahweh was in control. He was good, and He would be good to them. Now was the time to go on an adventure and see where Yahweh would lead them. Jarah couldn't wait to see the Promised Land. She could only dream about what it would be like.

"All right Yahweh, I'm ready to follow You," Jarah whispered. "Please, lead me to Your Promised Land."

THE END

MY RESEARCH

I have done a lot of research about ancient Egypt and the pharaohs and the timeline surrounding the exodus. Unfortunately, it seems that the more research I do the more confusing and contradictory all of the historical reports seem to be. And while the historical account does have some discrepancies, that doesn't mean that the Bible has any discrepancies. It just means that man in our fallen flesh hasn't been able to figure out the mind of God or how His amazing plan is woven throughout all of history. I'm sure we won't ever be able to figure it out. If we could, then God wouldn't be God, would He? God is sovereign, and one day everything will be made clear to us.

I am going to share with you some conclusions that I have come to during my study of ancient Egypt. I'm sure that while I believe and hope that my research doesn't contradict God's word, it might not be completely accurate. So while I will tell you what I've learned, I am not setting up this research as absolute truth but as something to consider and to make you think more about God's story.

You will notice that most of my story is placed in the Egyptian capital of Rameses, or in Goshen right outside of Rameses. If you look up cities in Egypt named Rameses today, you won't find any. That's because Rameses was the capital of ancient Egypt. Rameses is actually where the city of Tanis is today in lower Egypt. Rameses is listed several times in the Bible and is equivalent with the land of Zoan, which is also mentioned in the Bible. All of the Biblical references to these two places (Rameses and Zoan) say that the Israelites came out of Rameses/Zoan and went to Succoth, where they met up with the other Israelites who had been scattered abroad in the land of Egypt (in Memphis, etc.). That is why I use Rameses as the name of the capital Egyptian city. Rameses was only the capitol of Egypt during the 15th, 19th, and 20th dynasties. Most biblical historians believe that the timeline matches up with one of these dynasties.

I did a lot of research in the 19th and 20th dynasties, particularly settling on the 20th dynasty for two reasons. First, there were some golden chariot wheels found in the bottom of the Red Sea. (More about where the Israelites crossed and their actual route will be talked about in book two of this series.) The wheels were golden and some had four spokes, some had six. The four-spoke wheels were given up in the 19th dynasty and the six-spoke wheels took their place in the 20th. So there would have been some overlap with the chariot wheels.

Also, there are two Pharaohs whose lives seem to lend more towards the turmoil of the Exodus—Rameses the VII and Rameses the VIII. These both reigned in the 20th dynasty. Neither of their mummies have been found, and their tombs, though completed, were never used for them and were very modest. Both had short reigns and nothing much seemed to happen. Few things were erected, and there was obviously some turmoil (which would make sense if Egypt was completely devastated by all of the plagues). The Egyptians never wrote down tragedies in their records, and since little was said of either of these kings' reigns it would be good hint that something big happened during the time of one of their reigns. And lastly, during the reign of Rameses the VII it says that grain reached an all-time high price. Perhaps because the Egyptians had to import grain and had none of their own? However, since the Bible doesn't give any clues as to the name of the pharaoh, I decided it would be best to not name the pharaoh and his queen in my story. Their son, Rameses, is a truly fictional character. I chose the name of "Rameses" because I believe that one of the Rameses' was the pharaoh, and so it would make sense that the heir would have his father's name.

Research

All the description of the land, dress, palace, and the Hebrew houses was researched as a school project. Jarah's house is really the only one that was mostly constructed by my imagination. I also constructed the palace largely out of my imagination, with the basics of Egyptian architecture in mind as I described it. Below is a list of websites of my research. Also, all Biblical quotes and verses are taken from the book of Exodus using the New American Standard Bible (NASB).

Though all of this research is not something I would die for, I believe that it matches the Biblical account and makes sense historically. I hope this helps you all in your own research. I'd love to hear from you!

References:

Location of Rameses/Zoan:*
http://www.bibleorigins.net/ramesesmapavaris.html
http://www.aldokkan.com/geography/avaris.htm

*I do not agree that the Exodus was as early as the reign of Rameses the II as these websites state. I feel that the Biblical time-line and Egyptian history does not match up completely with Rameses the II. It is interesting to note that Rameses was the capital until the 21st dynasty when the Tanites took control of Egypt and started a new dynasty, moving the capital. Perhaps because the capital of Rameses was in such disrepair? Also, notice that the area of Rameses covered both the city of Tanis and Aravis, which is why ancient Rameses is often called ancient Tanis or ancient Aravis. Tanis and Aravis were united in the city and surrounding land called Rameses.

Two Possible Pharaohs:
Rameses the VII: http://www.findagrave.com/cgi-bin/fg.cgi?page=gr&GRid=7261715
Rameses the VIII: http://www.findagrave.com/cgi-bin/fg.cgi?page=gr&GRid=7261722

Clothing:
Egyptian Clothing: http://www.dragonstrike.com/egypt/cloth.htm
Hebrew Clothing: http://www.womeninthebible.net/3.3.Clothing_housing.htm

Architecture:§
http://library.thinkquest.org/10098/egypt.htm
http://www.biblearchaeology.org/post/2008/04/The-Royal-Precinct-at-Rameses.aspx**
http://www.egyptartsite.com/design.html
http://www.davidsongalleries.com/artists/roberts/roberts-egypt.php***

§I never really mentioned the pyramids in this book. After some research, I realize that the grand pyramids that everyone pictures when they think about Egypt are in a completely different city. Jarah's family could not have seen the pyramids. The Israelites were spread out all over Egypt, so Israelites must have been working on the pyramids, but not the Israelites in our story.

**Note: I don't agree with the timeline mentioned at the beginning of this page, but the pictures and descriptions of the palace are wonderful.

***Note: This website is one that my illustrator used for many of his illustrations and drawings.

ACKNOWLEDGMENTS

First and foremost I would like to give all the praise, glory, and honor to God. It was truly by His help that this book was written. There were several days when I sat down to write and I didn't know what was going to happen next! I prayed and just started writing. During those times some of the greatest parts and ideas of this story were written. I would look over my work the next day and think, "What? Did I really write that?" As a good friend of mine often says, "God does the work. I just hold the pencil."

Next, I would like to give my most heart-felt thanks to my family. First, to my Dad, Ken Auer, for reading through all my drafts, giving me ideas, and helping me through this process. Next, to my wonderful Mom, who is always an encourager and supporter of whatever I am doing. She has been my dedicated teacher and most faithful friend and mentor. I love you bunches! And also, I want to thank my amazing brothers, Caleb and Joshua. Caleb, thanks for being so encouraging and supporting and for posing for illustrations. Josh, thanks for looking forward to my book being written and for helping me know how to write the "little guys." You are a great little buddy. You both are always an inspiration to me!

For Hal and Melanie Young of Great Waters Press for agreeing to publish my book and for all the time and effort they spent with me getting my name out and coaching me through the marketing, editing, illustrating, and publishing process. I couldn't have done it without your help! Your experience and knowledge have been invaluable in helping me start the publishing journey. You and your family are an answer to prayer. Thank you for believing in me and my work.

A huge "Thank you!" to Mike Slaton, my illustrator. Thank you for coming on board very last minute and working so hard for this project. Thank you for putting up with all of the criticism my family and I sent your way and for trying so hard to please us. I know I can't even begin to count the hours of time you spent in researching, drawing, and sitting down and talking with me. I have really enjoyed working with you. You are incredibly talented, and this book would not have been nearly as good without your hard work and perseverance. Thank you!

I would also like to thank Crystal Hilton for all of the time she spent reviewing my rough drafts, listening to my ideas, and for all of her encouragement. You're such a wonderful sister in Christ, as well as a fabulous critic! Thank you so much!

A special thanks also to Saki Taylor for her time spent in reading my story and helping me make it better and cut out a lot of unnecessary details.

A big thanks to Gabriela Pothoven Morris for reading my story in its early stages and helping me develop new ideas and characters.

And Elise Allen, who helped me define the relationships between Ada, Paki, and Eitan, and helped me fine-tune my story. Thank you for your help!

Also Caleb Johnson, who helped me with some history research and checked my accuracy. Thank you for being a walking history textbook.

I want to thank the Twinklings Group (Mark Faggion, Emily Faggion, Ellie Faggion, Jacob Pendleton, Patience Sleep, Caleb and Matthew Young, and Trillian and Tristany Roper) for all their encouragement, inspiration, ideas, help with character development,

Acknowledgements

plot line, historical facts, and just for putting up with me in general. You guys are amazing!

And finally, I want to thank all of the many families and boys, girls, and young men and women who read my story through its many various stages, gave me their thoughts, and happily answered my questions. This story wouldn't have been the same without all of you! Thank you so much for the time you spent helping me!

The Brady Williams Family
The Adam Williams Family
The Irwin Family
Katie and Amy Lawson
Christiana DiLorenzo
Darian and Felicia Horvath
Julia Johnson
Lindy Meeker
Wilson and Victoria Brant
Emmy Slaton
Naomi Koch

—Hope Auer
May 2012

A Cry From Egypt

PRONUNCIATION GUIDE AND CHARACTER DESCRIPTIONS

(in order of appearance):

Jarah (JAY ruh): A twelve-year-old Israelite girl who is a slave in Egypt.
Ada (A dah): Jarah's good friend who is the hand-maiden of the Queen.
Queen: The pharaoh's wife.
Pharaoh (FAIR oh): The ruler over all of Egypt.
Eitan (EE tan): Jarah's oldest brother, who has a special interest in Ada.
Lemuel (Lem u el): Jarah's fourteen-year-old brother.
Acenith (ah SEE nith): An Egyptian girl who gets to know Jarah.
Bes (behs): Acenith's little brother.
Mubariz (Moo BAR iz): An Egyptian guard.
Paki (pah KEY): An Egyptian steward in the palace who befriends Ada.
Shayna (SHAY nah): Jarah's beautiful fifteen-year-old sister.
Raphael (Raf EL): Jarah's five-year-old brother.
Yanni (YAH nee): Jarah's baby brother.
Tirzah (TEAR zuh): Jarah's eight-year-old little sister.
Asher (ASH er): Jarah's father who believes in Yahweh.
Mariel (MAR ree el): Jarah's mother who believes in the Egyptian gods.
Amasai (ah MAY sigh): One of the Israelite overseers.
Amissa (Ah MEE sah): Ada's sister and Jarah's best friend.
Ezra (Ez rah): Ada and Amissa's fourteen-year-old brother.
Moses (Moe sus): The lost prince of Egypt who leads the Israelites.
Aaron (Air on): Moses' brother and mouth-piece.
Mayer (MAY er): Shayna's flirty friend.
Zephon (ZEF on): Another one of Shayna's flirty friends.
Tehara (Teh HAIR ah): The Egyptian cook at the palace.
Lexine (Lex EEN): Another Israelite maid who serves the queen.
Panhsj (PAN sjee): An advisor to Pharaoh and the prince's tutor.
Jaden (JAY den): Ada, Ezra, and Amissa's father.
Sanne (Sane): Ada, Ezra, and Amissa's mother.
Ammon (AY mon): Paki's father and a close friend to the pharaoh.
Rameses (Ram eh SEEZ): The crown prince.
Heru (He roo): An angry Egyptian guard.
Abalene (AH buh LEEN): Another maid in the palace.
Moselle (MO sel): An Egyptian maid in the palace.
Jahi (JAH hee): Paki's little brother.
Ife (Ih FEE): Paki's little sister.
Keket (KEY ket): Paki's baby sister.
Hathor (HAY thor): Paki's mother.
Manuel (MAN u el): One of Amissa's little brothers.
Manni (MAN nee): Amissa's other little brother.

Read a preview chapter of the second book in

THE PROMISED LAND SERIES

coming soon from Great Waters Press!

Jarah lay on her mat on the sand in the dark, watching the tent flap blowing back and forth in the chilling desert wind. She was mesmerized by what she glimpsed beyond the flap — a gigantic pillar of fire, reaching from the ground to the sky. It was so bright the glow dimly lit the tent, even from miles away. Her ears could barely make out the distant roar that came from the column of flame. The fire, swirling and dancing, seemed alive. It was hard, even frightening, for Jarah's twelve-year-old mind to grasp that Yahweh was actually living in their midst; that the one true God, Yahweh, had His presence in the pillar of fire that led the Israelites by night and the pillar of cloud that led them by day. She had only just begun to trust Him and follow Him as her Lord and she wasn't quite sure what to think of His awesome pillar.

She watched, awestruck, as the sun finally peeked over the distant mountains, making the white sand sparkle. The pillar of fire constricted, started to spin, and slowly grew darker and darker, changing into a column of cloud. Jarah groaned softly as she saw the cloud start to lift and heard a long, loud trumpet blast. That was Yahweh's signal to pack up camp and get ready to move on.

They had left Succoth in Egypt over a month ago and they had been traveling day and night ever since. Following Yahweh wasn't easy, but it was the only way to get to the Promised Land. Jarah slowly rose from the ground, her body aching and sore. She needed to wake up the other eight members of her family and help get everything packed into the wagon.

Preview Chapter

Jarah and her little sister, Tirzah, were riding on their donkey. Though it was still early in the morning it was already scorching hot. The Israelites usually traveled in the morning, stopped for the dreadfully hot afternoon hours, and then traveled on for several hours in the evening, often late into the night. Jarah was thrilled to see a change in the horizon early this morning. Looming up ahead of them were gigantic red cliffs, the throng of people crawling slowly past..

Jarah peered into the distance. Was her mind playing tricks on her, or was the pillar of cloud… turning around? Was it really going the other way and leading them off of the trading route?

Her oldest brother Eitan, sitting on the bench of their wagon, stood up slightly as if to look at what was going on. He sunk down again, whispered something to his fiancé, Ada, then called to their father.

"Father, the pillar seems to be leading us off the path and going back to the cliffs. Do you know why?"

Father, sitting on a donkey, struggled to see through the mass of moving Israelites. "I don't know, son. But Yahweh does."

Eitan nodded and goaded the oxen forward, his face grim.

It wasn't long before Jarah was urging her donkey into a deep canyon. Tirzah, sitting behind her, tightened her arms around Jarah's waist.

"Amazing," she breathed. Jarah could only nod. She had never seen anything like this. She'd only seen mountains from a distance. Almost the entire crowd was silent, observing the massive rocks in awe.

Hours crawled by as Jarah guided her donkey through the canyon, which appeared to be a dry river bed. They entered a second canyon, then another. Jarah's mind was in a whirl. It was like they were going through a maze. She was dizzy, and almost anxious. It felt like the cliffs were closing in on her. It was getting darker in the gorge, and the cliffs were getting higher. But suddenly, as they were coming over a small rise, they were out in the open. Mid-afternoon sunlight struck Jarah's face. They were on a huge beach, right in front of the Red Sea. Jarah and Tirzah drew in their breath sharply. The glistening, shimmering sea stretched out in front of them for miles and miles. Distant, enormous brown mountains stood up out of the other side of the sea.

A fresh salty sea wind blew into Jarah's face, making her thick brown hair whip out behind her. She inhaled deeply of the wonderful scent.

"Jarah? Come on! Keep up!" her mother ordered from where she sat curled up in the back of their wagon. "We're going to set up camp."

Jarah made the donkey trot over the sand after the wagon and the animals. Tents were already dotting the beach. Jarah glanced over her shoulder at the pillar of cloud, standing still at the edge of the sea.

Father led everyone towards the south side of the beach, away from the main crowd. In a few minutes Father, Eitan, and her fourteen-year-old brother Lemuel were assembling the tent. Mother was lying down in the wagon, listlessly. Jarah heard shrieks and squeals. Her little brothers, Raphael and Yanni, were running around and making a huge ruckus with their friends, Manni and Manuel. Jarah winced as Mother rose to her elbow. She knew what her mother was going to say.

"Jarah!" she barked. "Get your brothers this instant. And tell Amissa to get her brothers, too. I'm expecting a baby and I need my rest!"

Jarah sighed, handed the blankets she had been carrying to her beautiful older sister, Shayna, and then chased down the little boys.

"Raphael, Yanni, be quiet!" Jarah ordered, catching each little boy by an arm.

"But we want to play with Manni and Manuel," Raphael pleaded, trying to wrench away from Jarah's grasp.

"You can if we find someone to help me watch you. Mother wants us to go play somewhere else so she can rest. Remember, she's pregnant and tired. Manni? Where's your sister?"

Manni shrugged.

"I don't know."

"Jarah, is something wrong?" Someone spoke at Jarah's shoulder. It was Ezra, Lemuel's best friend and Ada's brother.

"I'm trying to find Amissa. Mother wants me to take the boys somewhere away from the tents, but I can't watch all—" Jarah was interrupted by Raphael finally managing to escape her grasp and dart away towards the ocean. "—all of them…" Jarah finished, sighing helplessly.

Ezra chuckled a little and gave her his familiar, teasing grin.

"I'll find my sister for you."

Preview Chapter

"Thanks," Jarah exhaled in relief. Ezra's dark eyes twinkled at her before he left to find Amissa. *He's so handsome,* Jarah found herself thinking. She gasped a little, realizing what had just crossed her mind.

Don't think that, she rebuked herself.

"Jah-Jah, come!" Yanni cried, dragging her towards the water. Jarah shook her head to clear her thoughts as she ran with Yanni to catch up to the other boys.

As the boys played in the waves, Jarah sat with her back against a boulder enjoying the luscious wind and the sprays of mist that hit her face. She closed her eyes, blissful. She felt Amissa sit down next to her.

"Shalom," Amissa said, softly.

"Shalom," Jarah replied. Then she whispered, dreamily, "Amissa, I could stay on this beach forever."

"It's lovely. But I feel it would get boring after a while." Amissa responded, softly. There was a moment's pause.

"Jarah, why do you think Yahweh led us here, so far from the road?"

Jarah slowly opened her eyes. The shadow of the rock stretched out before her. It was getting late. She shrugged.

"I don't know. Perhaps he wanted to give us a rest. We've only rested a few days since we left Succoth after our time of slavery in Egypt. The animals definitely need it."

"I suppose so..." Amissa's voice trailed off. Jarah looked into her face. Amissa's dark blue eyes were focused on her finger, drawing designs in the sand. She was worried.

"What's wrong?" Jarah ventured to ask.

"I just—I just have a weird feeling. I don't know. Maybe it's nothing. I just feel that something's going to happen. But I don't know what." Amissa struggled to relax her shoulders and appear casual. "I guess it's nothing. I have no reason to worry about anything." Amissa smiled weakly. Jarah smiled slightly back. She was starting to feel uneasy, too.

Raphael ran up to Jarah. His clothing was soaked and his thick black hair was sprinkled with water. "Jarah, we're tired of playing in the water. Can we go climb the rocks? Please, please, please?"

"Yes! Pwease, pwease, pwease?" Yanni entreated, jumping onto Jarah's lap.

"Yanni, get off. You're dripping wet!"

"Sowwy." Yanni penitently flopped onto the sand, his big brown eyes gazing into hers, begging.

"Please?" Manni asked, directing his pleading query to his sister, Amissa.

"I see no reason why not," Jarah said, rising.

"Well, it might be dangerous," Amissa fretted.

"Oh, we'll be careful. Very careful," Manuel stated. He tugged on Amissa's hand. "Come on!"

"Oh… all right," Amissa consented.

The boys yelled in delight and took off racing towards the cliffs, hundreds of yards away. The girls followed and by the time they caught up, the boys were already playing on big rocks and trying to scale the cliff-face.

"Don't go too high," Amissa warned.

Jarah was about to sit down on a rock when a noise from over her head startled her. Looking up, she saw three little lambs skipping up a tiny path on the cliff.

"Look at those lambs. I wonder if we should tell someone that they're here," Amissa said.

Jarah was about to agree with her when she suddenly gasped and said, "Amissa, those are our lambs! They must've strayed away. I've got to get them. They're going higher, and I'm afraid they'll fall!"

"Jarah, you can't!" Amissa cried, clutching her arm. "You'll get hurt!"

"I'll be fine. Go back and get Lemuel. I'll need his help. Take the boys with you."

"Can I help, Jarah?" Raphael asked, eagerly.

"No. Go with Amissa and find Lemuel."

Jarah clambered up the small path that the lambs had found. Some deer or goats or something must have made the path some time ago.

"Come on, little lambs. Come on down!" Jarah soothed as she approached them. But the lambs continued to frolic like they were playing a game.

"No! Come back!" Jarah exclaimed. The path was getting steeper. Jarah's heart stopped as a lamb slipped, but it quickly regained its footing and chased after the others. "Not higher!" Jarah exclaimed.

Preview Chapter

Soon, the path was quite narrow. There was barely room for Jarah to walk. Then she looked down.

Jarah heart leapt into her throat. She could feel blood pounding in her ears. She flattened herself against the cliff, trembling so hard she could barely stand. The bottom was far away, over a hundred feet down. Jarah was frozen to the spot in fear. She didn't realize she had traveled so high. She couldn't go on. She was panic-stricken. But the lambs—without them their family would lose some of their precious food.

Father would want me to get them. Oh Yahweh, give me courage, Jarah prayed, breathing hard. She tried to moisten her dry lips but her tongue felt like wool in her mouth.

She was just getting up the courage to continue when she heard a voice calling her name.

"Jarah? Jarah!"

"Lemuel!" Jarah called out weakly. Utter relief washing over her like a wave, making her feel faint. Her brother was coming to help her.

"Where are you?"

"Up here!"

In a moment, Lemuel came into view, climbing the steep path with the aid of his staff. Ezra was right behind him. Lemuel soon reached her.

"You shouldn't have come up here," he told her. His tone was a mixture of rebuke and worry.

"I'm sorry, I wasn't thinking."

"It's fine," Lemuel nodded. "You might still be able to help. We need to get those lambs."

But the lambs were more nimble than the humans and continued to travel even higher up the cliffs, soon reaching the top. Jarah gulped, trying hard not to look down. By now they must be hundreds of feet in the air.

The path, which had been switching back and forth along the face of the cliff, suddenly veered steeply upwards and widened slightly. Jarah drew in her breath. She could see the lambs on top of the cliff, but the final ascent looked very dangerous. Lemuel sighed, gently moved Jarah back against the cliff, and motioned for Ezra to pass them.

"Stay here, Jarah. This is too dangerous. Ezra and I will get the lambs and then come back to get you." Lemuel glanced up at Ezra who was slowly scaling the path. Lemuel's face was pale and alarmed.

"Do you understand?"

Jarah nodded in agreement, and Lemuel hurried after his friend.

"Look out!" Ezra shouted abruptly.

A large rock came rolling and bouncing down the path towards Lemuel. A scream caught in Jarah's throat as she clung to the cliff. Lemuel tried to jump out of the way, but it was too late. His legs were knocked out from underneath him and he was sliding down the hill, coming closer and closer to the edge of the cliff with every second. He was flailing, trying to grasp at anything, but there was nothing to stop his fall.

"Lemuel!" Jarah shrieked. She wanted to help him, but terror seized her and she couldn't move.

Lemuel was now sliding over the edge. He tried to grab at something—anything—and his hand grasped the edge of the cliff, breaking his fall. But Lemuel's grip was not firm. His fingers were slipping … Jarah couldn't breathe.

Out of the corner of her eye, Jarah saw something dash past her. The next instant Ezra was at the edge of the cliff. He fell to his knees and reached out for Lemuel just as his friend lost his grip. Their hands locked and Lemuel was saved, for the moment. But the ledge on which Ezra was kneeling began to crumble from the weight, and Ezra didn't have the strength to pull Lemuel to safety.

"Hang on, Lemuel. We'll get you up somehow," Ezra soothed as his head spun with thoughts and plans as to how he could help his friend.

"Ezra, what should we do?" Jarah cried.

"Just let me think!" Ezra shouted back.

"Ezra, I'm—I'm slipping! I can't hold on much longer!"

"You have to, Lemuel! Just a little longer. You can do it!"

"I can't!"

"Yes, you can!"

"Ezra!" Jarah screamed as a large piece of the ledge gave away.

Ezra focused hard on his friend. He had to get them out of this. But there was no hope left in Lemuel's white face, and Ezra felt his hold starting to fail.

"Ezra, just let me go! The ledge is crumbling and I don't want you to fall too."

"No, Ezra! Please, get him up!" Jarah pleaded.

"Ezra, it's the right thing," Lemuel urged.

"I… I…" Ezra didn't know what to do. He couldn't let his friend die, but if he hung on, they would both fall. Ezra's mind simply went blank. He had to do something, but what?

Please, Yahweh, Jarah prayed urgently, *help Ezra. I don't want either of them to die. Please, give him strength.*

א

"Eitan?"

"Over here, Ada!"

Ada circled a large rock and found Eitan sitting in its shade with a staff in his hand. He was watching their herd of sheep and goats which were happily resting on the clean sand. Looking up at her, Eitan smiled and motioned for her to take a seat by his side.

"I'm sorry to be looking like this," Ada apologized, blushing a little. She was wearing a plain brown dress that was patched and ragged. "Mother's washing the clothes in the sea, so…"

Eitan gently lifted her chin and looked tenderly into her calm brown eyes. "Ada, no garment could change the way I look at you. You're more beautiful every time I see you."

Ada smiled with pleasure. Her eyes glowed. They both sat in silence for a moment, just enjoying the peace, the stillness, and each other's company.

"Eitan, Father wanted me to ask you… I know it's a little too soon to talk about it, but… When do you think we should plan for the betrothal ceremony?"

"That's what I've been thinking about," Eitan said, letting out a long sigh as his eyes wandered over the flock. "I thought that it might be best to wait until we got to the Promised Land, but the journey has already taken more time than any of us had expected. Perhaps when we camp for a few days and have time to rest and plan… But I don't know. It might be better to wait. But I don't really want to wait…" His voice trailed off, wistfully.

"I can wait," Ada murmured. She looked confidently into Eitan's eyes and whispered, "I trust your judgment."."

Eitan smiled a broad, friendly smile. Gently, he squeezed her hand. "Well then, we'll trust in Yahweh, and see what He wills."

COLOPHON

This book is set in 12-point Adobe Caslon Pro with 14.4-point leading. William Caslon I (1692-1766) was one of the most influential early English printers and type designers, and his eponymous typeface was so beloved by generations of typesetters that it gave rise to the maxim, "When in doubt, use Caslon." Adobe's 1990 digital revival, by Carol Twombly, is one of the most graceful and versatile typefaces available to the modern digital typesetter.

The display faces are Eccentric Standard and Rockwell, an unusual pairing of slab serif fonts, a style known on the Continent as "Egyptian" for their unusual, exotic looks, although they bear little actual connection to Egyptian script or type design.

The main text was laid out in Adobe InDesign CS4 and CS6 with optical margins and glyph extension algorithms applied. Cover painting and internal artwork by Mike Slaton; external and internal layouts and typesetting are by John Calvin Young.

If you enjoyed A Cry From Egypt, you may enjoy these other books by Great Waters Press:

Raising Real Men
by Hal & Melanie Young

Christian Small Publishers
2011 Book of the Year

Are You Raising Boys?
You Are Not Alone!

A Practical Guide to Equipping the Hearts and Minds of Boys without Losing or Breaking Your Own

If this is God's chosen gift to us, then why does it seem so hard? How can we prepare these boys to serve God when we can barely make it through the day? Isn't there a better way?

The answer is yes.

"This is a book that every family should have..."
— J. Michael Smith, Esq.,
President, HSLDA

"**Just what the doctor ordered...**"
— Parenting columnist John Rosemond,
author of *Parenting by the Book*

"*Raising Real Men* is long overdue... this book is **a breath of fresh air.**"
— Dr. Tedd Tripp,
Author, *Shepherding a Child's Heart*

Find out more at http://RaisingRealMen.com and http://facebook.com/raisingrealmen!

Children in Church
by Curt & Sandra Lovelace

"THE CHILDREN ARE DISMISSED."

The enormity of this statement struck us hard. This says the children are dismissed. They will leave. There are no options. Out.

But what if you are beginning to think differently? What does the Word say about the role of children in the church? What will the other families think? How can you manage several children and get anything out of the sermon at all?

Curt & Sandra Lovelace share real, practical answers from their thirty years of ministry and as parents. This book will refresh you, strengthen you, and give you hope and help for bringing your children to the feet of the Savior in the body of believers in worship.

"This book is a must read for lay people as well as pastors and church workers. **All I can say is WOW!**"

– Adoptive Mom Homeschooling

"This book will answer all these questions and many more…along with giving you **amazing ideas on how to actually enjoy having your kids in church with you!**"

– Sacha at Home in the Trenches

Find out more at http://ChildreninChurch.com and http://facebook.com/childreninchurch.

Discounts are available for churches and other bulk purchases.

Need a Great Speaker?

Hope Auer, author of *A Cry From Egypt*, is available to speak on a variety of topics including writing, dads and daughters, and homeschooling high school in an unconventional way. Young audiences love Hope and get motivated to start working on their dreams of serving God now.

Curt & Sandra Lovelace, though residing in Europe, spend several months each year in the U.S. and are available to speak on children in church, homeschooling, special needs, prodigal children, the homeschool movement worldwide, and family-based discipleship. They are personable, friendly and funny with decades of experience.

Hal & Melanie Young are sought after conference speakers who routinely draw standing room only crowds with their mix of uniquely entertaining cross-banter and practical, powerful Scriptural principles. They speak throughout North America on raising godly sons, marriage, Biblical family life, homeschooling, and making the transition to adulthood.

John Calvin Young, eldest son of Hal & Melanie Young, is available to speak on economic and political issues, but especially on Christians in college. He explains in a winsome and inspiring way not just how to survive and keep your faith in college, but how to use the opportunity to have a very real ministry to fellow students.

Contact *info@greatwaterspress.com* to book any of these speakers.

CPSIA information can be obtained
at www.ICGtesting.com
Printed in the USA
LVHW021320280722
724617LV00007B/480